DON'T LOOK IN

TOM SARIC

Severn River
PUBLISHING

Severn River Publishing
www.SevernRiverPublishing.com

ISBN: 978-1-64875-017-5 (Paperback)

Knowing your own darkness is the best method for dealing with the darknesses of other people. —C.G. Jung

PROLOGUE

It was an unusual time of day for a killing. Murders were nighttime events, preferably in the rain, ideally during a thunderstorm. Not at noontime in the dead of summer, with the sun viciously beating down. Noon was for a quiet lunch in an air-conditioned kitchen, with a bowl of tomato soup and a slice of sourdough.

He sat in his car on the shoulder of the sunbaked two-lane road, holding the pistol in his lap. He ran his hand along the gun, savoring every groove and jagged bump.

Across the road, up a winding gravel driveway, the house stood atop the hill. Its fresh coat of paint reflected the sun, and a metal star hung above the porch door.

He opened the car, pushed the gun between his back and belt, and then put on a faded jean jacket. He looked both ways. No cars had passed in over ten minutes. The only sounds were crickets chirping in the ditch.

Six years of searching led him to this place. He'd searched, hoped, lost hope, and regained it over and over again. Stuck in that endless loop. He always suspected the man in the house knew. And he couldn't wait any longer. The man would tell him everything. EVERYTHING.

And once he got the truth, he would pull the trigger.

1

There's a place, deep in the woods, where the land slopes down to where the Persey River meets the Redway. The currents swirling at this juncture create a fisherman's paradise. Bugs bound over the cola-colored water. Brook trout wait below the surface, ready to pounce. I built a shack there from reclaimed lumber and would sit inside and listen. The steady hum of the flies, the water lapping, and the fish splashing would envelope me like a symphony. Week after week I'd traipse through the forest to this sanctuary.

On this day, I couldn't find it.

I slid across the ground, my ass bumping over tree roots, sending lances of pain down my legs. I leaned against a birch trunk, shifting until I found a position that didn't make my leg feel like it was on fire.

I tried my phone again, holding it up high like an offering to the gods, but still no service.

I looked at the horizon. Faint yellow lines clung to the bare trees on the hill. The sun had almost disappeared. The texture of the sky was changing, wisps of cloud coalescing into a jagged expanse. It was hurricane season. Tropical storms sent weather systems barreling up the Eastern seaboard, creating wet, windy autumn days and increasing the temperature above sixty.

I'd been through these woods a hundred times. I knew that every morning a family of deer drank water from the lake at that beach with the cube-shaped boulder. That the bald eagles fought over their spot on the top branch of a fir tree that broke in the storm last year. That the snapping turtles hibernated in the reeds by the tributary.

But three hours into my pheasant hunt it all became unfamiliar, as though I were transplanted across the world. Worse, transplanted to another planet. I might as well have been on Mars.

I circled back, retracing steps and searching for landmarks, but every turn was unfamiliar.

I lifted the phone, got to a hill. Too far. There was no cell tower for miles.

I scrambled down the hill, and my foot slipped on a loose rock. My hip smashed into a stump and I tumbled twenty feet, clawing and grabbing on my way down until I clattered into a fallen tree. My back seized. I crawled over the slick forest floor toward my gun, each movement sending a vibrating burn down my legs.

I commanded Anna, my dog, to go home, get help, before it got dark. I checked my watch. She'd been gone four hours. She must have made it by now.

It's been sneaking up on me for the past few months. I never know when it's going to happen. Maybe I should get it checked out. Fatigue has something to do with it.

The sun never seems to move as fast as when it's descending over the horizon. Blackness covered the woods, and there was no moon to give even a bit of light.

A pop. It echoed in the dark. Sounds were amplified. Maybe

nothing but a vole crawling over a twig, but it startled me like a gunshot.

I pulled my rifle close and held it across my lap. I tried to take a deep breath, but my chest felt stiff. Fear is nothing more than chemicals in the brain. Fear lives only in my head.

But my brain doesn't seem to be working like it used to.

I shouldn't have sent Anna out. I didn't even know which direction to point her in. Where did she end up? How could I expect her to find her way out?

The ground was cool. A wind picked up from the north and the gusts seemed to find gaps underneath my jacket. I flipped up my hood and let the wind howl around me. It was October, and luckily for me, tonight's temperature didn't drop below the sixties. Still, I was shivering, my arms rigid as I held my knees. Always be prepared. I guess I forgot that too.

They say most of man's problems are due to his inability to sit with his thoughts. That's all I've got now. My thoughts. And my gun.

There was a rustle to my left and then a branch snapped. A bird cawed somewhere in the distance. I loaded the rifle and held my breath.

I enjoy my own company. Funny thing, considering I preach connection as the antidote to society's problems. I'm a man of contradictions, I guess. Who isn't?

Gus Young. He lived alone and died alone. Maybe that's what they'd put on my tombstone. Died in the woods he'd been in a thousand times. Had a gun with him. Sent his dog away. Suicide, the police would think.

I didn't intend it to be like this. My move out here three years ago was my chance to regain some sort of peace. That's what I had told myself. Really, it was an attempt to run away. From the shame. The glares, the gossip. My coping rope was fraying, so really, I had nothing left to do but run. Running away from shame is impossible, though, because it lives inside you, like a cancer that chews away until there's nothing left. They say you can't run from your problems. That didn't stop me from trying.

Jung said loneliness didn't come from not having people around you, but from being unable to communicate the things that you find are important.

I guess Carl was never stuck alone in the woods.

A crack. A rustle. Feet stomping. I looked into the darkness around me but my eyes still hadn't adjusted. A bark. Anna's bark.

"I—" My voice cracked. I swallowed hard. "I'm over here."

Footsteps approached, cresting the hill ahead. A swinging lantern.

"Here. Right here."

A dark figure ambled down the hill smoothly, as though they saw every tree root along the way.

As the figure got closer, Anna sprinted to me, paws pressed against my shoulders, tongue licking my face. I let all fifty pounds of her onto my lap. I'd rescued Anna from a shelter in Bangor. She was a Pointer Springer Spaniel mix, which made her a great hunting dog.

Before I saw him I could smell him. Cigarettes and whiskey. He lifted the lantern. Thick glasses, tobacco-browned teeth, trapper hat. My neighbor, Herman O'Brien.

He spit. "Woods didn't swallow you up yet?"

"Still here. It seems I don't die easily."

"I know the feeling."

Herman was eighty-seven years old, thirty years my senior, but in better shape than me. He lived in these woods almost as long as I'd been alive. He passed me a flask and a plastic bottle of water. I put the latter to my lips.

"Take that first." He pointed at the flask. "It'll numb whatever ache you got. And it soaks in better when you're on empty."

It smelled like gasoline. "Home brew?"

He nodded.

I took a sip. I swear it burned a hole in my throat.

"You're gonna need more than that."

"What is this, ninety proof?"

"Don't know."

Herman watched as I emptied the flask. The burning made me forget all about the pain in my back. I guess that was the point.

"I thought maybe you were already into it and that's how you got yourself lost out here. But you're stone-cold sober."

Not anymore. I chugged the water bottle. I was thirsty, and had to get rid of the aftertaste.

"I got turned around. Then, with the trees bare, I seemed to lose my landmarks."

Herman's eyes narrowed behind his lenses.

"You're a straight line from your place." He pointed.

"It was getting dark."

"Doctor told me that if I start getting lost driving, he's gonna take my driver's away."

"Not the same thing."

"I told him like hell you will."

I glared at Herman. I didn't like his line of questioning. It was a simple mistake, getting lost, could happen to anyone. Herman held out his hand. I stood slowly, and his meaty hand wrapped around my forearm.

"Your back?"

"Yeah. I slipped down a hill. Old injury."

Herman reached in his breast pocket and pulled out a hand-rolled cigarette.

I shook my head. "Don't smoke anymore."

He laughed. "It's for pain. Doctor gave it to me for that. Says it's natural."

I took the joint and inhaled.

"Now let's get you home."

Rain was beating down on us by the time we reached my cabin. Day was breaking. The sun rising behind the thick clouds turned them green like an expanding algae bloom. Rain pelted the lake surface as waves crashed against the rocks.

"Have a good one," Herman said, and walked up my drive to the dirt road leading to his cabin.

"Do you want a ride?" Herman was my closest neighbor, but we were still separated by eighty acres of forest.

He shook his head. "Doc says I need the exercise."

Herman disappeared into the dark and I dug a key out of my pocket. I was still a bit high and drunk from Herman's moonshine, and the key slipped out of my hand and dropped into a puddle. I had just about lost feeling in my fingertips from the cold, and I couldn't feel the key in the cloudy water. So I ran my entire hand through the puddle until I scooped it up. I stuck it in the lock and tried to turn the deadbolt but it was already unlocked. Bridgetown was the sort of place where no one locked their doors. But big city habits die hard, and I had never forgotten to lock a door.

That said, I'd also never gotten lost in the woods.

I turned the slick handle and pressed the door open. Anna burst inside and I soon heard her lapping water from the toilet. I flicked on the light, stepped inside, and scanned the room, part of me fearing I'd see someone. I didn't move for a good thirty seconds. When I was satisfied I was alone, I leaned the

Remington next to the door and took off my boots and jacket, then walked past the kitchen into the den.

Even though Meg had taken me to the cleaners in the divorce, she left me with enough of a nest egg to start my new life as a hermit. I found pictures of the original cabin on the shores of the secluded inlet on Origa Lake. It was dilapidated, and I could hear raccoons scurrying underneath the deck when the agent first showed me the place. But the cabin was secluded, had an old boat launch, and at sunset the view across the lake was spectacular. So for those reasons I decided it would be mine. That, and I couldn't afford anything better.

I took possession in one of the rainiest springs I had ever experienced on the East Coast. The roof also leaked, which meant I not only had to replace that, but the pine shiplap on the right side of the house had rotted and had to be ripped out.

But I got it the way I wanted. Metal roof, pine interior, and floor-to-ceiling window overlooking the lake. I even had a basement where I kept my gun collection. On the west side of the place I added a den and lined the walls with shelves I milled from local birch. I piled my books and vinyl records on top—all I took with me when I sold our place. I kept my original editions of Freud's *The Interpretation of Dreams*, Jung's *Modern Man in Search of a Soul*, and Anna Freud's *Defense Mechanisms*, which my mother gave me. These leather-bound books sat on the shelves alongside records of country greats Kenny Rogers, Loretta Lynn, and The Highwaymen.

I popped in a wood stove, which made the cabin seem complete. No TV, radio, or newspaper. No neighbors. Just man and nature, the way God intended.

In the den, I wrapped myself in a crochet blanket, then opened the wood stove and stacked it full of split wood and kindling. I got the fire going before returning to the kitchen and putting a kettle on the wood stove. A bit of hot tea would help me sober up and relax, and hopefully ward off the chill that ran through me.

Then I opened a drawer, found my bottle of pain medication, and dumped the last two into my palm. Time to stop by the pharmacy for a refill.

I grabbed my rifle and went to the basement. I'd collected rifles over the past few years, keeping them downstairs in my lockable gun cabinet. However, I'd been keeping it unlocked because last month I'd forgotten the combination. I'd had to destroy the lock and buy a brand-new one.

My cell rang. I searched for it in my jacket. Few people knew my number, and those who did knew to call only if it was important. Sheila Gustafson was one of those people. The head of customer service at Buck's Hardware. And also my secretary.

"Gus," she said. "Where on earth have you been? I've been trying you since yesterday afternoon."

My phone started buzzing, alerting me to new voicemails that must have been picked up now that I was back in service territory.

"Long story, Sheila." I held the phone between my cheek and shoulder while shoving a few more logs into the wood stove and closing the door.

"Are you okay?"

"I'm fine. Always fine."

Sheila worked at Buck's for twenty years and pretty much ran the place. If anyone in Bridgetown needed a snow blower chain in June or a dock lift in December, Sheila was their first call. And she would get it done. People in town got so used to her solving their problems that they began calling her for advice. They asked for help with anything from toilet training their little ones to figuring out if their husband was running around on them. They treated her like an on-call Dear Abby.

I moved out to rural Maine with the intention of keeping to

myself. But I needed supplies for my cabin, so I ended up going to Buck's almost daily. When Sheila learned what I did in my past life, she set me up with the people who needed more help than she could provide. She found me an office. She managed my calls. The woman could handle most anything, so three messages was unusual.

"It's Wanda," Sheila said. "She's been calling. I've tried to talk her down, but she's begging for a session."

I looked at the clock. "I could possibly make it in for eleven. What's the problem?"

"She was just rambling on the phone, she..." Sheila stopped. "Gus, really. She's a handful. And she doesn't even-"

"What did she ramble about?"

Sheila huffed. She didn't like when I cut her off but I didn't want to get into it with her. Sheila always made sense. But sometimes, I just didn't want to hear it.

"Something about her brother. Something about him being back."

Clients usually embellished when they wanted to be seen. Sort of like when I have a sore throat for a few days I tell the doctor it's been a week so I will get a course of antibiotics. Say what will get you in the door.

But Wanda's brother had been imprisoned for ten years. And her testimony had buried him.

"Randy's back. Okay, I'm coming in. I'll be there by ten."

2

I parked in the lot in front of Buck's Hardware, my truck taking up a space and a half. The fall mums were already on sale, stacked on display crates on either side of the entrance. After a quick look at myself in the rear-view mirror, I wiped some dirt from my cheeks and pulled a few dried leaves from my beard.

The sign above the door announced that Buck's had been operating in Bridgetown since 1950. When the original store was bought out by the House Hardware national chain, Buck Thompson was able to negotiate to keep his name on the sign. The new name was Buck's House Hardware. I walked through the sliding door, my steel toes tracking mud, and headed for the back of the store. Linda stood behind the cash register, so I waved and thanked her for the ginger molasses cookies. She'd brought them to me last week as a thank you for helping her six-year-old son beat his fear of Bloody Mary.

Sheila was waiting at the customer service desk, wearing her sharp red smock with a *20 years of service* pin. Since it was Monday, her hair was freshly curled.

"She's already inside," Sheila said, looking over her reading glasses at me.

"Your hair looks nice."

I walked past the customer service desk and pushed through the swinging utility door. To the left was the public restroom and door to the warehouse. I took a right down the fluorescent-lit hall to what had once been a utility closet.

When Sheila had asked me to see one of her cousins who was struggling with the grief of losing her husband, I needed a place to see her. So Sheila cleared out one of the utility closets and threw a couple of clearance Adirondack chairs inside. I saw her cousin in the closet that smelled like bleach twice a week for eight months.

Then word got out, so my caseload increased. Sheila decided to renovate the ten-by-ten room. She replaced the fluorescent lights with a warm yellow pendant light and floor lamps. She painted the room burgundy and accented it with oak moldings. She found a few original oil paintings and some prints at the annual town yard sale for under five dollars a piece. She got one of her nephews to hand-carve a bookcase out of rosewood. When Sheila was done, the former closet looked better than my former office, which was a thousand square feet and overlooked Boston Harbor. I wondered what my former colleagues would say if they saw what I was doing now. I wondered what Alistair would say.

Sheila wanted to have my name embossed on the door, but I insisted on keeping the *Utility* sign. It was inconspicuous. Clients could anonymously walk in through the swinging door and leave through the back door. No one would see them come and go, and if they did, they would think they were just heading to the public restroom.

I pushed the door open and flopped down in my plush velvet chair. A jolt of pain ran up the side of my spine as I settled into the cushion.

Wanda sat across from me, looking like hell. She glanced at

me and then hunched over, looking uncomfortable in a skin-tight tangerine dress cut six inches above her knees. A large ornate silver cross with a turquoise stone in the center dangled from her neck. Not that Wanda was religious; she inherited the cross from her grandmother. Her hair was messy, and mascara tracked down her cheeks. She smelled of cigarettes. Wanda looked down, as though she was cowering from me.

I sat and said nothing, taking a moment to settle and bring myself into the room. Although Wanda was still hunched over and crying, I could sense her eyes on me, checking me out, assessing me, taking my emotional temperature.

No doubt Wanda had noticed my boots, the mud caked on the sides, my grimy hunting jacket, my dirty fingernails. A woman like Wanda only needed a split second to size someone up. She was perceptive like that. It's how she survived.

I felt no urge to speak. She had called the session, so it was important that she begin. For me to speak would only serve to infantilize her. Wanda was learning to be an adult, and there was no need for me to do things for her that she was entirely capable of.

That, and Wanda had done the doubled-over, wounded-fawn routine with me a dozen times over the years. We had worked through it, brought this behavior to her conscious awareness. She understood that this was one of the games she played. Part of her now consciously knew what she was doing.

"I told myself not to call." She kept her head down and swiped at her nose with a tissue. "I already know what you're going to say."

She made eye contact for a split second and then flicked her gaze downward.

I still said nothing. I could sense that she was projecting something onto me, casting me into some role from her past. I had a pretty good hunch who I was emotionally representing for her, but telling her that now would be useless. She needed to get there herself.

"Put on your big-girl panties and face it."

I've never said that. Never said anything remotely like it, in fact.

"Maybe you wouldn't say it like that." She smiled a bit and looked at me, seeing if I would reciprocate. I gave a muted smile. She was using humor, an age-old way to channel aggression. But under that anger was pain, so she was making a joke to try to avoid feeling that way.

"I've been outside, in the parking lot, since, fuck, I don't know." She looked at her watch. "Four a.m. Jesus. Just sitting there, smoking one after another. Thinking about you, what you're going to say when Wanda comes in with even more drama. Drama Queen is what I am. Queen of the Drama Queens. Drama Empress."

She laughed, but only with her mouth; her eyes didn't join in.

"I sat out there for four hours agonizing about what to say, and here I am, pouring my heart out, Gus, and you just fucking sit there."

"You look sad."

"Sad? That's all you got, the great Dr. Gus Young, world-famous shrink?"

I gave a half shrug. It was all I had. Part of me wanted to say, "Cut the crap, Wanda, you're projecting me as one of your abusers, seeing if I'll hurt you like they did. I'm not going to do that, so let's get past it and deal with what is happening right now." But I'd be saying that out of anger, which would only reinforce her projection.

"I'm fucking mad. Mad 'cause I count on you and you just look through me. Maybe the papers were right about you. Fucking fraud."

That was vicious. It had only happened a few times, clients bringing up the story from years ago that was picked up by the *Boston Globe*, *New York Times*, and *Washington Post*. I wanted to lash out and correct her. Tell her what really happened. But therapy wasn't about me. It was about Wanda and she was projecting hard. She was testing me to see if I could withstand the force of her anger. She wanted to know if I could be trusted to contain her rage, her sadness, her pain without turning on her the way almost everyone else in her life had.

"You feel as though you don't matter to me."

"Matter? You've got your list of patients, you sit there, listen to them yammer on for fifty minutes, and then go hide in your cabin."

"What would it look like if you did matter?"

That question hit something deep. Her eyes widened and shifted. She sighed.

In Wanda's world, she was nothing, she barely existed. Her mom, a drug addict, let all sorts of men into the home who had their way with Wanda. Her dad, perhaps the only person who thought she mattered, killed her mom in a fit of rage when he walked in on her in bed with their neighbor. Poof. Just like that her mom and dad were gone. Wanda ended up raising her little brother and selling herself to make ends meet. She was considered a town pariah. So, yeah, she never mattered.

"I felt so stupid last night. I was supposed to meet Joe at eleven over at Schooners. I showed up, sat at the bar, ordered a beer, nursed it. Eleven came and went."

Wanda shook her head. She wasn't projecting anymore. She was more clearly identifying the source of her anger now. I was no longer the lightning rod.

"There was some guy, over in the corner all night, drinking his face off, playing with his phone. Never seen him before, but I could see him checking me out."

She leaned forward, pulling her shoulders back and pushing her breasts out. She ran her hands down her thighs, watching as my gaze drifted to her hands.

"Is this too much for you, Gus?"

Wanda was still projecting. But now she was testing to see if I would take out my own anger on her when she was acting vulnerable. Wanda tended to channel her pain either through anger or sex.

"Is what too much?"

"This story. Is it getting you too hot under the collar?"

I had to admit to myself that Wanda was attractive. She had gorgeous wavy long hair, a petite, curvaceous frame. But what Wanda didn't understand was that attraction didn't equal sex. That love didn't equal sex. That two people could have an affinity for each other, care for each other, but not hurt each other. Her parents never taught her that.

"Wanda, as we've discussed before, my interest isn't in the content of what you talk about, but in why you say it and why you behave in certain ways. And I can't help but sense that part of you wonders, maybe because I'm a man, whether I'll hurt you. It's like you're seeing how close you can get your hand to the fire without getting burned. But I'm not going to hurt you, no matter how hard you try."

She looked at me, and I saw a flash of the Cheshire grin before she continued.

"Then midnight. Then one. Still nothing from Joe. So I started calling, over and over, but he's not answering. Probably knows it's me. So I go over to the guy in the corner and ask for his phone. Call him from a different number, right? And guess what?" Wanda's eyes lit up. "Joe picks up on the second ring. Son of a bitch." She shook her head while pressing her tongue against her teeth. "I let him have it. And you know what he says?" Her eyes welled up. "'We're going to try and work it out.'"

I gave the classic, "Hmmm."

"Work it out?" Wanda's voice was loud. "Two years. Two years of promises, Gus. He told me. He told me he loved me. He told me he would leave her. And just like that. Like-"

"You didn't matter."

"Yeah." She looked at me with hurt eyes. The first genuine emotion I'd seen in her today. "For a while I thought I was something."

I let the grief hang there. She needed to feel that loss. The loss she'd been living with her whole life. The loss of self.

"He was so charming. Every time he came over, he brought me my favorite flower: gladiolas."

Two years ago, Wanda got a prominent client: Joe Barrington. Joe was married and a former college football player. He came from a prominent local family.

He was also the town mayor.

Wanda was giving Joe something he wasn't getting at home, and he was giving her a feeling of being something. She stopped charging him. Joe made her all sorts of promises, and it seemed that he was going to leave his wife. At least it seemed that way in Wanda's fantasy.

"What was I thinking? Town mayor moves in with local whore?" She shook her head and laughed. I didn't smile. "You'll never guess what happens next. The guy who gave me the phone says—wait till you hear this one. 'While he's working it out, in the meantime,' and he shrugs!" Wanda laughed again. "He seemed sweet. And I was mad. So I did what I do best, Gus." Wanda looked away and picked at her nails.

"And then you called me."

"I just needed to feel safe."

"That's what you've been searching for."

"No, no, it's not like that. It's Randy. He got out. And he called me. He wants to meet."

Things started to become clearer. Her brother, Randy, got involved with some local drug pushers. Ten years ago, in the midst of a turf war, he killed one of them and buried the body. Wanda's testimony had been pivotal in sealing his conviction.

"What did you say?"

"I said yes. But how do I know if he's mad at me? I had this dream last night, while I was in the car sleeping in the parking lot. I'm back in my mom's trailer. In the bed reading an Archie comic. I'm scared, though, trying to block out the noise. I can hear screaming, mom yelling 'no.' But I'm paralyzed. I hear footsteps coming and I just freeze up. The door opens and it's Randy. Not little Randy, but Randy today. He's got a shotgun pointed at me. His finger tenses up. Then I wake up."

"You feel guilty about Randy."

"He was my brother. My little brother. I raised him, Gus. I was like his mom... and I gave him up."

"You had no choice."

"I could've shut my mouth."

"And then what would've happened to you? To him?"

"He was such a good little kid." Wanda covered her face and sobbed. "I fucked him up."

I could feel myself being pulled into her guilt. It was overwhelming. In therapy I always preferred interpretations over advice. I wanted clients to find their own answers. But sometimes it pays to be direct.

"Wanda, Wanda, look at me." She looked up, head stooped, but made eye contact. "You were put in an impossible situation. First, as a teenager, you were basically raising a little boy by yourself. Then, having to tell the truth not just to save yourself but probably him too. What you did was show strength and courage. To be frank, most people would've folded a long time ago. But not you. You don't give up. You always have hope. That has never died. And you know what? That's what I admire about you."

Wanda gave me a childish little grin. Pride. "Thanks."

I truly admired Wanda; none of that was bullshit. And for all the digging and interpretation I do as a therapist, sometimes it helps just to tell the truth.

"So should I go see Randy?" I stared at her. "I should go see him. I want to. You won't say anything about Joe to anyone, right?"

"Wanda, we've talked about this. This is confidential. The only time I'd say anything is if you told me you were going to go and kill yourself or someone else. And even then, I'd say the bare minimum."

"What if I tell you I've killed someone?"

"That's confidential." I raised my finger. "Unless you say you'll do it again."

"I killed Hoffa."

"I always thought so."

Confidentiality is the prerequisite for effective therapy. How could I expect people to discuss their deepest secrets, the ones that eat at them, if they couldn't trust me? The therapy room was sacred. Even if it was a utility room.

Wanda got up and walked to the door. "Who do you tell your secrets to?"

I shrugged and turned away.

"I can tell you have secrets too."

3

I finished writing the notes on my encounter with Wanda in a coil-bound notebook with her initials on it. I kept two records of my sessions with clients in these notebooks, one in a yellow notebook with their full name on it and the other in a baby blue one with only their initials. I wrote more details in the blue, not only to help me remember what was said from session to session but also to allow me to notice relationship patterns that repeated themselves over the course of years.

I lifted the painting of a mountain lake that looked like a Bob Ross duplicate off the wall. Behind it was a combination safe anchored to the concrete outer wall where I kept all my active client notebooks. No one, not even Sheila, knew the combination. My patients' secrets were locked away. Most shrinks keep their notes in charts and store them inside flimsy file cabinets that their secretaries have easy access to. Not me. The notes were for my eyes only, and the only purpose they served was so that I could provide better therapy. But lately, it seemed I needed my notes more and more to jog my foggy memory.

I twisted the knob and pulled the handle. It wouldn't open.

I tried again. The number didn't work.

I closed my eyes and took a deep breath, trying to calm myself so that I could remember the code.

Karen's birthday.

The bolt didn't budge.

People forgot things all the time. Combinations, phone numbers, zip codes. We were inundated with numbers, so it was understandable for our memories to slip some of the time.

Backward.

The safe clicked and whirred and swung open. I filed Wanda's notebook, then shut the safe and hung the painting back up. I'd barely slept last night in the woods. Lack of sleep was the most common cause of a fuzzy memory.

I walked over to the customer service desk where Sheila stood, filling out a ledger.

Behind her stood Brian Gallant, store manager and the late Buck Thompson's grandson. "Sheila, I don't mind you doing this for the doc, but first I need the orders for the-"

"I've already taken care of the orders for the Hebb farm, Brian, and left them on your desk for your signature."

"Okay."

Sheila rolled her eyes at me as Brian left for his office. She could probably handle the work of five people and still get home and make a five-course dinner.

"Still not charging her, eh?"

"No."

"Just saying that you're putting a lot of work into that one, is all. The freebie, white knight stuff is admirable. But now she is 'asking' for emergency appointments?"

"It's how it is."

"You're going to start resenting her."

"Sounds like you're doing it for me."

Sheila took issue with my seeing Wanda pro bono. She was partly blinded by Wanda's reputation in town as the riff-raff, the troublemaker. That, and Sheila quilted with Lorna Barrington. Most people in town speculated that something was going on between Good ol' Mayor Joe and Wanda. But Lorna seemed oblivious. Maybe willfully so. And the people who whispered about it generally fell into one camp: it was Wanda the seductress's fault.

Good ol' Joe just couldn't resist. Wanda? Well, she was just a status seeker.

Sometimes people like Wanda just need someone in their corner.

"Just be careful with that one, is all," Sheila said.

Part of me wondered whether Sheila was jealous of Wanda receiving favorable treatment with me. Sheila and I had gone on a couple of dates shortly after I moved to Bridgetown, but she called it quits. I was too much in my head, she told me. It was for the best, I think, because we now had a solid working relationship.

"You've got a new guy coming in at one-thirty, so don't be late for that one."

"Any background on him?"

"Nope. Just that his name is Doug Steele and he paid up front for ten sessions."

That was good. Sheila handled all the payments for my practice. She was constantly after me to raise my rates, because they were less than half what other therapists in the area were charging. But I just needed enough to get by. And that way more people who needed help could get it. The deal was that I worked only in cash. I didn't want insurance companies getting between me and my clients.

"Here's last week's billings, after overhead. Keep some for yourself. You don't need to keep sending it to her."

Sheila didn't approve of my sending money to my daughter Karen. She hadn't spoken to me in three years, and Sheila thought she was just taking advantage of me by accepting my money.

Sheila began counting out the bills by laying them on the table like a bank teller, the way she always insisted. I put my hand up to stop her, as I always did. "I trust you."

Sheila stuffed the pile of bills into an envelope. I reached over to take it when I heard, "Where is he?"

The voice came from the front of the store. I could hear Linda, the cashier, say, "Who, sir?"

"Don't pretend. The shrink. That quack. Ah, forget it."

I could see the top of a man's head over the stack of paint cans as he stormed up the main aisle. He wore a black trucker hat with the words "Support East Coast Militia no. 14." I still couldn't believe there were at least thirteen other militias. His shoulder-length white hair fluttered behind him.

"There you are." He locked on me and marched forward.

He wore a down-filled vest with no shirt underneath, leather pants, and motorcycle boots. He carried a stack of papers in his right hand.

"Thought you could get away with this?"

"Hi, Ned."

"I'll see you later," Sheila said, raising her eyebrows and mouthing "good luck" as she turned and walked away.

"You're here, pushing these drugs to people—government-funded drugs that came from Johnson & Johnson. And Dave Johnson, up the road, has been working with the deputy mayor to get these drugs handed out, making us zombies so that Buddy Getson and his boys could run roughshod over us."

"Ned."

"And we gotta live with them because we ain't going for at least another sixty years. You know who predicted that?"

"Yes." Ned had told me about his end-of-the-world theories before.

"Newton. Anyway, I'm out here this morning on the 59, scraping a deer off the road into my truck, and who do I see?"

"I don't know."

Ned glanced over both shoulders, then leaned in and whispered with cigarette breath, "Davey Johnson at Buddy's place."

Ned leaned back, arms crossed as though he had just closed the case.

He gave himself the moniker "Night Hawk" Ned and he sees it as his duty to patrol the county roads overnight, looking for roadkill to clear off the asphalt. It was a good public service too, as it likely prevented a lot of accidents. Ned would then incinerate the carcass and make decorative pieces from the antlers.

He also had a paranoid personality disorder. He'd never met a conspiracy theory he didn't like, and he was constantly adding to the list.

The sad truth is that this paranoia was just him attributing his internal fear outwardly onto others and the world at large. While he seemed angry and in control, inside, Ned was a terrified man.

"Gee, Ned, that's scary."

"You're damn right you should be scared." Ned motioned to the door. "Just saw that whistle-blowing whore leaving here. Getson's got you marked." He made the hand gesture of a gun.

"I'm not that scared."

"Why not?"

"'Cause it sounds like he'll come for you first, Ned."

Ned looked at me with suspicion and then shook his head. I'd taken Ned on as a client two years ago and had seen him on and off ever since. He had gotten into an altercation on the highway because he was directing traffic so a family of Blanding's turtles could cross. A tourist got frustrated and tried to drive through Ned's makeshift road block, so Ned chased him down and pulled the man out of the car before putting the car in neutral and rolling it into a ditch.

The court sentenced him to community service (which, Ned argued, he was already doing) and anger management classes. We were still working on the anger bit.

Every month or two, Ned would barge into Buck's and launch into some sort of tirade. It's gotten to the point where I can usually defuse the situation with some lighthearted humor.

Some people might fear the six-foot-five giant. I don't. At least not anymore.

"Let's have a look at what's got you concerned."

"Like you don't know."

"Ned, let's stop dancing around the issue here. Because, frankly, I don't know what the hell you're talking about. You haven't told me."

He laid the papers on the customer service desk and took a deep breath. "Last month, you charged me for four sessions, but that couldn't be. Because I was away for one week, at the boat show, so I missed that session."

I looked at his receipts and indeed saw four from last month.

"How many people are you doing this to? Corruption, corruption everywhere."

I called Sheila and eventually she came in from her office, holding a half-eaten salami sandwich and shooting daggers at me for dragging her into this.

"Sheila, it looks like we have overcharged Ned here. He was only here for three sessions last month, but we charged him for four."

Sheila took one glance at the receipts and turned them around so that they faced Ned and me.

"Gus, Ned. You'll notice here at the top, there is a date. What does it say?"

Ned and I exchanged glances.

"Gentlemen, these invoices are two years old, they're not from last month. But Ned, you are right, you still owe on this invoice, so thanks for bringing that to my attention."

Ned quickly piled up his invoices.

"You two just make sure you stay honest. There's crooks all over this town."

Ned walked out and I picked up my envelope of cash.

"Just make sure you're back by one-thirty," Sheila reminded me.

"Danny, right?"

"Doug," Sheila said. "Oh, and the pharmacy called, they need you to call about a script." She handed me a sticky note with a phone number.

I made my way to my truck, hopped in, and turned up the music. The Highwaymen blared from the ten B&O speakers surrounding me. Before I moved to the cabin, I realized that getting rid of my '89 Volvo would be a good idea, especially during the winter, as getting through the snow-filled back-country would be near impossible. My initial thought was to get a simple, small, used quarter-ton pickup.

But just before I went to the dealership, I ran into my ex-wife's current man, her former personal trainer, at the grocery store. We had an awkward exchange, him in his muscle shirt, his veiny biceps taunting me as he stuffed a bunch of organic kale into his basket. I stood there with a box of ready-made chicken wings from the deli. I felt emasculated standing next to him. Small.

So I went to the dealership and bought the biggest fucking truck I could find.

A black Ford F-450 XL 6.7 V8 engine, 400-horsepower gas-guzzling beast that was so heavy it required two extra rear tires just to move it. With my new baby I could drive over boulders, up cliffs, through streams. I could rip out stumps, haul tree trunks, and run over anyone who got in my way.

Maybe one day muscle man would step in front of it.

Johnny Cash's baritone filled the car, singing something about how the desert was his brother. Somehow it made sense.

I took the envelope of cash, counted out half, and put it in another envelope marked *Karen*. No return address. I still had no idea if Karen knew it was me sending her the money. Or if she even got it. Sheila thought I was silly, sending a grown woman money. Call it parental guilt.

I noticed the sticky note to call the pharmacy. I assumed it had something to do with the antipsychotic for Wes Tate. He was one of my patients with chronic schizophrenia, who spent his days roaming through the county collecting scrap metal. Pharmacy often called to clarify because he was on such a high dose, but it was the only dose that kept him functioning. I picked up my cell phone and dialed.

"Hello, this is Renee."

"Hi there, Renee. This is Dr. Gus Young, I got a call regarding a prescription?"

"Oh, yes. It's regarding - wait, are you a Waylon Jennings fan?" She sang along with the radio for a verse. "I'm sorry. So sorry, that's unprofessional."

I turned down the sound and found myself smiling. "It's okay, it's a great song."

"Not as good as 'Silver Stallion.'"

"'Good Hearted Woman?'"

She chuckled. "I'm sorry, I'm just a big country fan."

"'I'm a Ramblin' Man.'"

"Are you now?" She cleared her throat. "Sorry, Doctor. You're probably busy. I was calling about a prescription."

"Yes, sorry. Who is it regarding?"

"Oh, it's just your pregabalin renewal. It's ready for pick-up."

"Great, thank you. You can call me Gus."

"Okay. Gus."

"Renee."

4

Buck's parking lot had filled up by the time I got back after lunch, so I had to park at the far end to find a space big enough for my truck. I looked at my watch. I was already five minutes late.

I took a quick sip of my coffee and bite of my sandwich and ran across the parking lot, narrowly avoiding a few trucks backing up without looking. I hated being late for sessions, especially the first meeting with a client. Every move in a therapy session sets norms and expectations. Every motion, every darting glance, and every sigh are deliberate forms of communication from our unconscious mind. There are no coincidences. Everything means something.

As I walked past customer service, Sheila didn't look up.

"He's already inside."

"Thanks."

"It's Doug."

I had been treating an eighty-year-old client for an almost lifelong history of panic attacks that started after her brother died in front of her after falling off a horse. Her name was Violet. Except I had called her Rose. She never corrected me.

After six months of weekly sessions, she called Sheila to tell her that she was no longer coming in. She said she was insulted that after nearly thirty visits I had never gotten her name right.

Since then Sheila reminded me of clients' names every single time.

I pushed through the swinging door into the back hallway. Beside my office door was a mop and bucket full of dirty water that smelled of chlorine.

I took a breath, still winded from the run inside, and opened the door. Doug stood by the wall, his back to me, looking at a framed print of an old world map. He was about five foot eight, shaved head, and had a long earring dangling from his right ear. He couldn't have been over fifty-five, but he had the thick skin and deep creases of a person who lived hard. He turned around, chin down, and looked up at me with his hand on his belt buckle.

"Neat map."

"It's from 1440," I said. "A print, of course."

"Half the world's missing."

"They didn't know that back then. I find it a good reminder that we never know as much as we think we do."

"About what?"

"About anything."

"Like me?"

He leaned forward, as though by getting a closer look at him I would suddenly recognize him. He unbuttoned the cuffs of his jean shirt and began rolling them up like he was readying himself for a fight. His arms were covered in tattoos. Judging from his tough-guy facade, Doug was testing me. He wanted to know if I could handle myself in front of him. Or if I was weak.

"I know even less about you. Except that your name is Doug." I smiled. "And that you've paid for ten sessions."

"Always about the money, ain't it?"

"Hey, we've all got to get paid."

Doug wasn't done testing me for weaknesses. In his world, it seemed, people only did things for selfish reasons. Judging from the way he dressed, the way he carried himself, the way he spoke so directly to me in only our first session, I realized he was trying to home in on any vulnerability that he could detect. So that he could exploit it.

Doug was a psychopath.

He held my stare for an unnaturally long moment, but I didn't flinch. Then a big smile broke across his face.

"Ain't that right, brother."

He sat down in my chair, which would have been obvious to him because my notepad and prescription pad rested on the stand next to it. Beside the opposite armchair was a box of tissues. Doug was testing again.

I stood, lips pursed, until he looked up at me and feigned surprise.

"Oh, this is yours?"

I nodded.

He hopped up with his hand raised deferentially and sat across from me. Doug shimmied into the chair and sat with one leg across his lap, his elbow on the armrest, and his chin in his palm.

"They say you're the best."

I had to give it to him. Beaming smile. Eyes alight. The man had charisma. But I could sense that something lurked below the surface.

For years, I'd been flown across the globe for court-ordered assessments of some of the most notorious serial killers to poison the earth. None had the sophistication and eloquence of Hannibal Lecter; quite the opposite, in fact. But they all had one thing in common: an utterly compelling appetite for controlling others. To work with a psychopath, I had to show that I couldn't be exploited.

"They lie."

Doug laughed, but it was hollow. He looked at the floor.

"I used to be the best," he said.

"Used to be?"

"Life catches up to us."

It finally felt like Doug was getting into what brought him in. I decided to press him a bit to see how much confrontation he could tolerate.

"Life caught up to you."

"Fuck, yeah." Doug put his hand to his forehead and shook his head slowly.

"That's what brought you here?"

"That's why I came to see you. Hoping to resolve this shit."

"This shit?" He was being vague, circling around whatever the issue was.

He sighed deeply, then threw up his arms.

"How do I know I can trust you? I'm just supposed to tell you everything and trust that you keep it secret. Just unload here?"

"That's sort of how it works."

"And then what? You just keep all these secrets. Write 'em down on your notepad? Where does that go? Who sees that?"

Doug's hand was shaking, his voice too. He had something to share. Something shameful. Maybe something illegal.

Psychopaths don't show shame. They don't show guilt. My initial impression of him might have been wrong. Perhaps Doug was simply being guarded.

"Let's be clear here. This won't help you if you don't trust me. And you won't be able to trust me if you think I can't keep a secret. So, Doug, listen to me. What you say in here, stays in here. I don't repeat it. My notes are kept in a safe. Only I know the combination." I tripped over those last words.

"This holds with only three exceptions."

Doug nodded in anticipation.

"If you tell me you are going to leave here and kill yourself or someone else."

"That's it?"

"Or if you tell me you will hurt a child."

"Of course," Doug said quickly, then hesitated. "What if I tell you I killed someone?"

I treated this as a hypothetical. Immediately questioning him on that would cause him to shut down. If I was going to get him to open up, I had to keep things light. "Doug, you could tell me you're the Zodiac Killer. As long as you tell me you're done, it stays here."

"Jesus, you must've heard a lot of shit."

"Don't worry, I have a shitty memory anyway."

That made Doug laugh. The truth was that I have had people tell me they had killed their mistress, carried out a hit, and committed war crimes. Holding these secrets ate away at their psyche, like a cancer of the mind. Talking about it was the only cure. Sunlight is the best disinfectant.

"So, can we cut the crap and you tell me why you're here?"

"Just, I guess I've just been running. And it stays, you know? In here." He tapped his forehead.

"For how long have you been running?"

"Forever. Dad died, maybe after that? Yeah, maybe then."

Doug dove into his life story as patients often felt the need to do. His dad died on their farm while building a barn; one of the trusses collapsed, crushing him as Doug looked on. Doug slipped into petty crime, then started stealing cars, then started running with a biker gang. Each time he alluded to drug running, assaults, or "taking care of" someone, he glanced up at me, as though he was checking to see if I would rat him out.

But he was avoiding a topic. He was describing all of this

hard living but offering very little emotional material to hold on to.

"Doug, you said you're here because you want to stop running away. But for the past twenty minutes you've been running in circles, telling me your life story. I get the sense that you're still running from what you need to tell me."

Doug glanced up at the ceiling. His eyes quivered and then welled up. His jaw trembled and he doubled over, sobbing.

After a minute, he sat up and looked at me with hurt eyes. "I feel like I killed her. My baby girl."

I let his words sit inside of me, like a lead weight in my gut. I was wrong about Doug. He was no psychopath. He was experiencing immense grief.

"Your daughter died?"

He nodded.

"I didn't actually kill her. She took care of that. Three years in May." He bit his lower lip. "I met a good woman, and we moved to this nice cottage with a big property that backed onto a beautiful creek. And then we had Maddie. She was everything to me. But that life never left me, you know? I didn't protect her, didn't teach her right.

"She got into drugs. When she was twelve it was weed and alcohol. Coke at fifteen. Then she started hanging with thugs."

My heart was beating. Doug was around my age, with a daughter. A daughter who couldn't have been much younger than Karen. Things went downhill and he wasn't equipped to stop it.

"I kicked her out. Told her to clean up. Teach her a lesson, you know?"

I knew.

"Three weeks later, she's dead on a street corner. Overdose. Died alone. Like a dog."

Doug was silent, staring out into nothingness. His tears had dried up.

"Don't know, Doc, if you have kids. But if you do, keep 'em close."

Doug stood up and pointed at the clock. "Time's up. I'll see you next time, Doc."

The door shut and I sat in my office, alone. For the first time in a decade, I wept.

5

At ten that night I drove to the brand-new Irvine gas station off the main highway. Only a few cars passed by, usually full of teenagers heading out to the woods to drink. The massive blue sign stood atop a hill, on a big patch of asphalt cut right out of pristine forest. Blinding overhead LEDs lit the pumps, and posters advertised a free sixty-four-ounce fountain drink with a fill-up. It was the newest thing in Bridgetown.

I parked at the furthest end of the lot, in the shadows just outside the fan of light. I tried not to think about my session with Doug, and how he had let his daughter slip away. Doug's story wasn't that different from mine. For years my psychiatry practice took priority over everything, including my marriage and parenting. I told myself I was building a reputation, and I was making money. Eventually I'd make up for the lost time. I'd send her to Woodrow Wilson, her dream school. She'd hung her hat on that too, as though we both agreed that in exchange for my deadbeat parenting, she would get a first-class Masters degree in international relations. When I'd destroyed my reputation and squandered away almost everything I'd earned, we had nothing left to hold us together. Just hurt feelings and animosity.

I had two envelopes of cash, one for Karen in the driver's door pocket and the other wedged in the space between my seat and the middle console. I wrestled with the idea of adding a return address to Karen's envelope. Or maybe including a short note. Just to get the communication going again. Maybe enough time had passed.

But why me? Why should I be the one to end this standoff? She was getting my money. Isn't that all she really wanted?

Headlights drifted across me and a gold Pontiac Sunfire pulled up. The car was left running as Buddy Getson got out, all five foot four of him, the top of his head barely visible over the passenger side window.

"Open up," he said with a grin that was exaggerated because of his lamb chop sideburns.

I unlocked the door, and he made full use of the running board and handle to heave himself into the passenger seat.

"Let's see it." He held out his hand, waggling his fingers.

I passed him the envelope.

Buddy pressed the map light on and counted out the bills. "You're short."

"Eight hundred a week, Buddy. That's what we agreed."

"We also agreed you'd pay weekly. But you missed two weeks. So the price goes up. A grand."

I shook my head. I had no recollection of agreeing to a thousand a week. "We agreed?"

"You came begging to me, okay? 'Cause you couldn't handle yourself." He pointed a finger in my face. "So I did you a favor, Gus. Now, where's the rest?"

My left hand dropped and my fingers touched Karen's envelope. He didn't notice.

"You still playing? Huh?" Buddy turned away in disgust.

"Jesus. You know you've gotta get some help, man. You've got problems."

"I'm not playing." I held his stare to show that I wasn't lying. "No. I'm done."

"I want my money. Consider this notice. Next week, your interest rate goes up. Twelve hundred a week."

Buddy threw the door open, jumped out, and slammed it. My fingers were still on Karen's envelope.

I didn't want to be involved with a guy like Buddy Getson, but I had little choice. After the divorce, I needed to blow off steam, and exercise and whiskey just weren't cutting it. I'd always liked cards, and hell, I was good at it too. I could read people; noticing their tells came easy. I'd gotten carried away with it before, and Meg would later say it was why she left. Alistair said it was why I had to leave the institute. Those were just easy outs for them. They wanted to get rid of me.

I dug myself deep and needed money, so I turned to Buddy. After Wanda's brother Randy had killed Jimmy Getson, Buddy inherited his father's criminal enterprise— running the local dealers, trafficking coke and meth, stealing and stripping cars, and loan sharking. He was also Wanda's pimp, not that Wanda needed much protection. Buddy was the kind of psychopath I hated—unsophisticated and insecure, which made him especially dangerous. But he gave me cash at a reasonable rate.

I'd learned to control the urges, the cravings. Sometimes. I flipped down the sun blocker and felt for a cigarette. Checked the armrest console. Glove box. Nothing.

I grabbed my wallet and went into the convenience store. I stood behind a teenager in an oversized shirt that said "Bridgetown's Finest." He bought three bags of Doritos, two liters of Dr. Pepper, and a pouch of chew. He was one of Buddy's thugs. Bridgetown's Finest was the local street gang, one that

Buddy managed. I always wondered if they understood the irony of the name.

I stepped up to the counter.

"Box of Marlboro Lights, please."

The clerk turned around, looking through the cigarette drawer. I rarely smoke. Just sometimes, I need that little hit.

"No more Marlboro."

"Anything light, then."

As the clerk dug through the drawer, my eye was drawn to the lotto max jackpot. Forty-eight mil. If I won, I'd be able to get Buddy off my back, but I'd have to keep my winnings secret or he'd never stop harassing me.

It was just a dollar. This was an addict's rationalization, but it seemed harmless. I knew a snowflake could turn into a blizzard in no time. I squeezed my hands together until they turned white.

The clerk put a pack of Du Mauriers on the counter.

"Anything else?"

Screw it. "A lotto max, please."

As he printed my ticket, I felt my heart deflate. I told myself it was just one. Just one more.

I stuffed the cigarettes and ticket into my jacket pocket and turned around.

"Hey."

A tall woman was staring at me. My gaze drifted up. She wore yoga pants that accentuated her long, slender legs, and a lilac running jacket. She swept her wavy blonde hair behind her ears and smiled with eyes that seemed to sparkle.

"Gus?"

I nodded. Barely.

"It's me." A playful grin. "Renee. From the pharmacy."

I let out a strange sound that was half sigh, half laugh. I couldn't stop staring.

"Right, I re-I remember you."

A pregnant pause. Her eyes followed my hand into my pocket.

"It's okay," she said. "I indulge every once in a while too."

I shrugged, wishing she hadn't seen what I had bought. I pointed at the milk jug she was carrying. "Looks like you're making healthier choices than I am."

"Well, I have this rule. I don't smoke alone."

"And I can't smoke all of these."

She paid for her milk and we stepped outside. We walked around the store, sneaking past the propane exchange like we were teenagers, and lit up on the curb. We both started coughing as we took our first drag.

"I guess that's a good sign," I said.

We sat on the curb and talked for another hour. She explained how she had divorced and stayed in New York City until her daughter was an adult, and then decided she needed a slower pace. She'd applied at pharmacies across Maine, and Bridgetown was the first to call.

"So, how did you end up here?" she said. "You were pretty prominent there, sir, those big cases across the country." I raised my eyebrows at that, wondering how she would have known about my past. "Yeah, I looked you up after we talked. Google."

"Can't hide anything anymore, eh?"

"Why bother?"

I took a breath, trying to figure out what to say. "The short version is, well, I wanted to slow down."

"... And the long version?"

"It sort of reads like a Greek tragedy. Actually, maybe like a Coen brothers' film. But it's more of a third date kind of story."

"Dr. Young, you are kind of smooth. Are you asking me out?"

"Is that a yes?"

She nodded. We exchanged phone numbers and I headed to

my truck, feeling light. It had been years since I'd hit it off with a woman and it felt like something sparked inside of me.

She walked off the lot and up the shoulder of the highway. I drove up beside her.

"You're walking?"

"It's just two miles up that way. My car's in the shop."

"C'mon," I said. "I'll give you a ride."

She hesitated.

"Just a ride." I held up my hands. "There are coyotes at night. It can be dangerous sometimes."

She hopped in. Hank Williams was playing and we sang along together.

"Tell me, how does a woman like you get into classic country?"

"My daughter. She always used to listen to Johnny Cash. Even John Denver."

"What does she listen to now?"

Renee paused for a second, staring straight ahead and lost in thought, then looked at me. "Sorry, I was just looking for my place. Yes, she still listens to the same music. It never changed."

"That's great."

"So what do you like about this town?" she said.

I shrugged. "A lot. It's quiet, the people are nice, but I have my space. Everyone minds their business in a nosey kind of way. But the pristine nature around us here, it's spectacular. There's this place..." I trailed off. I wasn't sure I wanted to let anyone know about it.

"A special place? It sounds neat; you don't have to tell me if it's like a secret fishing hole or something."

"No, it's nothing like that. It's just this place I like where these two rivers meet, the Persey and Redway. Everything just feels good there for me. It's hard to explain."

Renee smiled. "I know what you mean. There's a beach

down in South Carolina I used to visit. When I'm there everything just, just-"

"Stops."

"Yes! Like time stands still." She drummed on the dashboard.
"I'll tell you what. One day when you trust me, you take me to
your special spot and then we'll go down to mine."

"That sounds great."

The music stopped abruptly as my phone began to ring over
Bluetooth.

Herman was calling. I pressed talk.

"Herman, hi, is everything okay?"

"Well, I wish I could tell you it was. But..."

"What's wrong?"

"There's smoke comin' out of your place. Firefighters are
already there."

"Anna?"

"Don't know. But I'm heading over."

"Shit."

"This 'as been one helluva day for you, neighbor."

6

High beams on, I made it through the serpentine dirt roads to my cabin in record time. I thought only of Anna, squeezing the steering wheel to stop my hands from shaking. Renee had grabbed my right hand, interlocked her fingers with mine. She said little. Whispered "It'll be okay," but through the back-country dark I could see she was worried we'd arrive to a dead dog.

By the time I reached the edge of my driveway, I had received three phone calls from Sheila, letting all go to voice-mail. Nothing she was calling about could be more important than getting to Anna.

My driveway was a quarter mile long, cut through a thick forest full of birch and oak trees. Red, blue, and white lights from the firetruck and sheriff's cruiser flashed through the sticks. Smoke billowed above the trees and the stinging smell of melted plastic expanded.

Halfway up the driveway, Deputy Debbie Parks stepped in front of the truck, her hand out, motioning for me to stop. I threw the truck in park and jumped out.

She must have noticed my panic. "Fire's under control, Doctor."

I ran past her toward the front door. One of the firefighters stopped me.

"We can't let you inside, Doc."

I tried to walk around him but he put his arm out to block me.

"Is Anna in there?"

"We haven't cleared the cabin yet. Was anyone inside?"

"Anna." My voice rose. The entire addition—my den, my library—was covered in black soot, and the roof was steaming. Windows were shattered. "Anna was in there."

He looked perplexed.

"His dog," Renee said from behind me. "Anna's his dog."

"Oh," he said, relieved. "I thought you meant there was a person inside. Your dog's fine."

He directed me around the fire truck where another firefighter sat on the back bumper, holding Anna on a leash.

I ran over, and the second she saw me, she began straining on the leash, jumping up on her hind legs and barking and whining. She broke free of the fireman's grip. I knelt down and let her jump all over me. Anna had been with me through the divorce, leaving the institute, through the media harassment. When I came home one day thinking I'd finally had enough, she lay down over my feet, her chestnut-brown eyes gazing up at me. I couldn't bear to leave her.

"I wish someone loved me like that," Renee said, putting out her hand to let Anna smell her. As she gave Anna a rub behind the ears, I smiled.

"She's lucky," the firefighter said, taking a swig from a water bottle. "Fire was contained to the library. Didn't spread to the rest of the house. Found her curled up under the bed."

"Same place she hides during a thunderstorm."

"That probably saved her from the smoke too."

"Any idea what started the fire?"

The young man shook his head. "I just put 'em out." He turned toward an older firefighter holding a clipboard. "I leave that to the captain."

The captain was talking to Ernie Weagle, the county sheriff, until Ernie broke off and called Debbie Parks over. They talked for a few minutes and then walked toward me. Ernie stayed a few feet behind Debbie and avoided eye contact with me. He had been a patient of mine for a few months for a matter he was deeply ashamed of. Ernie liked to wear women's underwear and stockings. His wife was the only person other than me who knew about his fetish, and she was fine with it. But Ernie wasn't.

It took three months of digging for him to come to terms with his fetish. Though judging from his bowed head and stooped shoulders, he might need more work.

"Shaken up, Doctor Young?" Debbie said.

"I'm fine now. Anna's okay, that's what matters. And please, call me Gus."

"We just need to take a statement from you." She pulled out a postcard-sized notepad. "Routine procedure."

"Sure, yes. Shoot." Anna was running around excitedly, getting tied up in the leash.

"When were you last in the house?"

"Um..." I puffed out my cheeks, then looked at my watch. I couldn't quite remember the earlier part of the day. I felt Ernie, Debbie, and Renee staring at me, so I tried to act as though I was distracted by Anna. I crouched down, untangling her leg twisted in the leash.

"Just ballpark is fine," Debbie said.

Wanda, I remembered; I'd left to see Wanda. I pulled my phone out of my jacket, flicked through my call records, and saw the morning call from Sheila. "Around nine, nine-thirty."

"And you slept here last night?"

I was having episodes, but they were sporadic. Due to insomnia, really. The police would make too much of my getting lost in the woods. So I decided to lie. "Yeah, I was here. With Anna."

Debbie went through the morning routine, and I kept my statement vague and nonchalant. I'd learned through years of court testimony that being too definitive only led to trouble. Police and lawyers were trained to look for inconsistencies to discredit people. Leaving myself wiggle room, and providing statements that couldn't be proven false, was a form of self-protection.

She asked if there were ever any minor fires in the house. If I'd come back midway through the day. I didn't know Debbie Parks, I'd only seen her with Ernie around town. I heard she had moved from Vermont a year ago. Mid-thirties, hair pulled back tight, she had a certain gravitas about her. I sensed there was a lot more turning in her mind than she let on.

"Ever any issues with leaving the stove on. You know, getting preoccupied and forgetting? The iron maybe?"

I could tell by the way she looked at me there was more to these questions than routine procedure.

I pursed my lips and shook my head.

She tapped her pen on the notepad. "Okay."

"Is there an issue? Maybe you want to ask me something directly?"

I decided to challenge them, in part because I wanted to demonstrate that I had nothing to hide. Debbie deferentially turned to Ernie, who still had his head down. He took a second to realize Debbie was asking him to step in.

Ernie pulled at his nose a couple of times and wiped his mustache. "Doctor, eh, Gus. Firefighters think, well, they were questioning a kettle that was left on the wood stove. Some papers were left nearby. A notebook or something."

I stopped petting Anna, and my mind drifted to making tea that morning before rushing out. I didn't recall leaving a notebook out.

"It happens, Gus. More than you'd think. We get busy, you know, other things on our minds. Just wondering if it's happened before." He cleared his throat. "So that you're safe."

"I had an emergency call, so I was rushing out. You can ask Sheila Gustafson, she'll confirm. I must've forgot about the kettle." I looked at Ernie and then Debbie. "And no. It's never happened before."

Ernie nodded quickly, as though he just wanted to escape.

"You'll have to get yourself somewhere to stay," Debbie said. "They have to block off the place until inspectors come through to clear it. Get the insurance company in. You might have to take down the addition."

I sighed. I had been meticulous in getting my den just the way I wanted. I could get that back, but the books and records were irreplaceable. Maybe some of them could be salvaged. I was glad that the rest of the house was intact, because I kept old patient records in the basement cabinets.

"Can I get some stuff from inside?"

"Not today. Once they clear it, then okay. It'll probably take a day or two."

Debbie and Ernie walked away, and Renee put a hand on my shoulder. It felt comfortable.

"I once forgot to turn off the iron, left home, and didn't remember until I was on a toll bridge toward Baltimore. I U-turned through the booth, cars honking, people rolling down their windows and swearing at me. I drove the two hours home." She touched my cheek and gently moved my head so she was looking into my eyes. "And you know what? When I got in my driveway, I remembered that my iron broke a month earlier."

I laughed with her. She'd said what I needed to hear.

Herman O'Brien wandered up, wearing chest waders and pointing at Anna with his cigarette. "The ol' girl made it."

"Thankfully. Thanks for noticing the fire, Herman. It could've been worse."

"Hard not to notice with a smell like that."

Renee shifted uncomfortably next to me. I sensed she wanted an introduction. "Herman, this is Renee. Renee, my neighbor, Herman."

Herman held the cigarette to his mouth and took a drag while checking out Renee. She reached her hand out but he didn't reciprocate. "And who would you be?"

"Um, I don't, I don't." Renee looked at me, flustered. "His, um, friend?"

"Well, nice to meet you, Gus's friend."

Herman then turned away from Renee and faced me, as though he was trying to cut her out of the conversation.

"A kettle, eh?"

"That's what they say."

"Afternoon tea gone wrong?"

"Morning tea."

Herman squinted and tilted his head. "Hmm. Could've sworn I saw you leaving this afternoon."

I felt my knees almost buckle. My memory of the entire day was fuzzy. Could I have forgotten coming home mid-day?

"What's an ol' guy like me know. The days. The times. They all blur together." He flicked his cigarette butt into the woods. "You're gonna need a place. I got space."

Herman's home is what happens twenty years after a married man becomes widowed. He hadn't ever cleaned the place properly. He exclusively used disposable plates and cutlery. The toilet and shower looked like they had never been scrubbed.

"Herman, thanks, but I think I'll stay in town, closer to work. I don't want to impose."

Herman shrugged. I'm not sure he really wanted me there any more than I wanted to go.

"Maybe your friend here will offer."

Even in the dark, I could see Renee blush.

"If, if you want, I mean-"

Every part of me wanted to go home with Renee. But I reminded myself that fires that burn bright quickly run out of fuel. My ex-wife taught me that.

"You are both kind. But I'll get a room in town."

She opened the door and offered to take his jacket, but he declined. They had been expecting him, she said. That was unfortunate. He didn't think anyone else would be home. It was supposed to be just the two of them, talking. This complicated matters.

He stared at the back of her head as she led him down a hallway. Through her brown curls, he could see its shape—boxy, with hard angles attached to a short, thick neck. He'd aim at the top of the neck, just above the fat fold where the base of her skull met her spine. It would take one shot, clean through the spinal cord.

They passed through the kitchen. The counters were wiped down and shiny. The stove looked brand new, and a tea towel hung perfectly square from the oven handle. A steaming tea pot sat on a hot plate. She didn't offer him any.

She led him into a room that was all windows, without blinds of any kind. The sun blared down, forcing him to give his eyes a few seconds to adjust. The windows looked out at a forest. No neighbors could see inside.

The room already had the overripe-fruit smell of death. He turned the corner and saw the hospital bed facing the window. He hadn't expected that. He slowed his stride and approached cautiously.

The young man lay on the bed, twisting awkwardly against a stack of hard-looking pillows, his legs tangled in a white sheet. Bald, his skin ashy and pale yellow, with dark gray rings around his eyes.

The man's eyes slowly swept over him. "You weren't expecting to see a dying man, were you?"

7

I had a restless night, but still managed to sleep late into Tuesday morning under the tightly tucked-in sheets at Bridgetown's Comfort Inn. I was woken up several times through the night, first by a youth hockey team stampeding through the halls, then a car alarm in the parking lot, and finally a midnight romp between the couple next door. Afterward my aching back prevented me from settling into a comfortable position, but I was determined to catch up on some much-needed rest. Despite not having my medication with me, I managed to find a position that minimized the pain.

The situation reminded me of the weeks I spent living in a hotel after Meg asked me to leave. The mattress at the Hyatt was larger, sheets softer, pillows fluffier. The room was pristine, decorated with airy whites and creams, unlike the taupes and maroons of the outdated Bridgetown motel. But it felt the same. I was alone in that luxurious room too. No one had come to check on me then, except for the room service guy looking for dirty dishes. No one checked on me here either.

I thought of Renee. Maybe I could call her. Maybe she cared where I was.

I should have invested time into my relationships. It seemed like the therapy couch was all that mattered. As though I was a voyeur interested only in the inner workings of other people's lives, oblivious to my own world slowly eroding and washing away. Everyone important in my life had moved on while my back was turned.

Leaving the institute was probably a blessing. I'd completed a court-ordered assessment on Anthony Cruz and deemed him a low risk to re-offend. Two months later, after he raped and killed two more women, my credibility and reputation were destroyed. And with the media fervor and relentless investigative reports that followed, the institute's standing as the most prestigious psychoanalytic school in the world was irreparably damaged. My colleagues avoided me in the halls. I was taken off committees. Even my mother, a former president of the institute, began to doubt my skills as an analyst. "It seems you have some blind spots to work out," she had said. "It's unusual for someone of your standing to have such shortcomings."

But I realized that I was no company man. My path to psychiatric fame was preordained by my mother. She'd even named me Gustav. Not because we had a Germanic background. No, I was named after one of the psychoanalytic greats: Carl Gustav Jung. No one but her called me anything but Gus.

The truth was that psychiatric prominence wasn't what I wanted. And as much as I looked up to Alistair—my mentor and Trustee Emeritus of the institute—I wasn't interested in having theories and therapies named after me. I didn't need the attention. The attention is what buried me.

There was a quiet knock at the door. Then louder.

"Yes?"

"It's me," Sheila said. "Let me in."

I rolled off the bed, then, realizing I was wearing nothing but underwear, ripped the sheet off the bed and wrapped it around myself. I waddled over to the door and flipped the deadbolt.

Sheila was carrying a box of donuts, two cups of coffee, and a yogurt cup. A plastic bag hung from her elbow. She sniffed and then made a sour face.

"Lordie, lordie, Gus. You didn't shower last night?"

I shook my head. "I came here and basically passed out. But I love that you're looking out for me."

She passed me a coffee and put the yogurt, donuts, and her coffee next to the TV stand.

I flipped the coffee tab open and deliberately smelled it before taking a long sip.

Sheila set the grocery bag on the bed and began pulling items out of it.

"A toothbrush and toothpaste, deodorant." She held the stick out in front of me. "You might want to use that now. Shaving cream and a razor."

That made me laugh. Sheila hated my beard, and any chance she got she tried to make it clear that she wanted it gone. "What are you hiding behind that thing for?" she would say.

"I figured you needed a change of clothes so I stopped at Frenchie's." The local consignment store.

She pulled out a crisp white dress shirt, tweed blazer, and navy slacks and laid them out on the bed. "I figure you can look more the part."

"Are you trying to change my image?"

"Hunting jackets and steel-toe boots fit in a bit better with the loggers. Oh, that reminds me." She pulled out a pair of shiny caramel-colored loafers complete with tassels.

I stood over the bed, examining my new wardrobe. "You know, Sheila, these could be the very clothes I donated when I first moved here."

"I don't think it'll kill you to clean up a bit, is all."

I had a soft spot for Sheila. She always looked out for me, like an older sister, which is probably why it never worked out between us.

When I'd moved to Bridgetown, I shed the Sigmund Freud style of clothing, the wooden demeanor, the facades, and the arrogance that was drilled into me at the institute. I was done being anything for anyone else. I was going to be me. Sheila was straightforward like that too. She said what she thought. And according to her, I was a slob.

"All right, sweetheart." I tapped her cheek like I was a chauvinist from the 1950s. "For you."

I flipped open the donut box and took one with sprinkles. Sheila sat in the chair and sipped her three-sugar, three-cream coffee, examining me for a little too long.

"What?" I said.

"Are you okay, Gus? I mean truthfully."

"Yeah. Fine."

"It's just that, well-"

It wasn't like Sheila to beat around the bush.

"Sheila, spit it out. I'm a big boy."

"Just the stove, the fire. Coming in late, dirty sometimes." She sighed. "Ever since you moved here, you just haven't slowed down. Going and going. And I know you're the expert, but, well, you've got to take care of yourself. Cardiologists get heart attacks too."

"Are you worried I'm having a breakdown, Sheila?"

"I just wonder if things are catching up with you."

I'd never seen Sheila quite like this. Worried. It was unsettling, because Sheila didn't get worried.

My biggest asset in my work had always been my memory. I could remember details, and little inconsistencies in stories that emerged over time. I could use that to my advantage to help people see their own contradictions so they could address them. With my memory slipping, I felt like I was navigating in the dark without a map.

I'd thought about seeing my doctor about it, but the episodes came and went. And if he got worried he could get my license to practice revoked. The most likely explanation was that I was under stress and not sleeping well. In a few months, everything would be back to normal.

"Sheila." I touched her forearm, attempting to project confidence. "I'm fine." I took a breath and checked in with myself. I thought of Renee. "I actually feel happy."

She nodded and smiled. "You do seem a bit happier today. Maybe burning down a house is some sort of cleansing?"

"Maybe." I laughed. "The kettle. It slipped my mind. Happens to everyone."

Sheila hopped up and waved at the clothes. "Okay, I'll leave you to it then, darling."

"Thanks for the mothering."

"Don't forget to use soap."

I shook my head and went for my second donut.

Sheila stopped at the door.

"Gus, where were you last evening?"

"What do you mean?"

"When I called you. You didn't answer. And you weren't home. You never go out."

I thought about telling Sheila about Renee. But she wouldn't approve of me spending half a night with someone I'd just met in person. And I still wondered whether a part of Sheila would be jealous. But that wasn't worth getting into.

"I needed gas, so I went for a drive. Just thinking."

"Okay. Do you want me to cancel your first appointment?"

"Who is it?"

"Your couple. The Barringtons."

I thought of my meeting with Wanda and wondered if I had the energy to deal with Joe and Lorna Barrington.

"No. Don't cancel. I'll be there."

8

Lorna Barrington was wearing a light blue dress, cut low at the ankle and high at the neck, with lace on the collar. Covering up was decent. She had her hair pulled back into a tight bun and her hands crossed on her lap. Lorna was always astonished when I brought up her rigid posture. This was no surprise, as her puritanical upbringing had brainwashed her into believing that she had to behave as though she were living in 1765.

Joe sat on the chair next to her, legs splayed, wearing a black blazer and dress shirt open at the collar. His wavy hair was slicked back, and his thick mustache was neatly trimmed just above his lip. He viewed himself as Tom Selleck. The *Magnum, P.I.* one. I had to admit, he could pull it off.

"I was preparing for the show on Sunday. I have been selected, gratefully, for a stand, about six feet long, at the farmers market. The committee at..."

Lorna was the type of client I dreaded working with, especially when I was tired. Everything about her was stilted. Her language was slow and deliberate. Her movements were rehearsed and robotic. Her voice was monotone with a steady, unwavering rhythm.

Truthfully, I could see why Joe would stray. There was simply no way she could satiate his desire, and a guy like Joe always got what he wanted.

"Lorna, I get it," I said. "You were preparing for your quilt show. But we are here to work on you and Joe-"

"I am getting to that."

Joe rolled his eyes as Lorna kept talking. Our sessions revolved around her mindless stories that were only obliquely related to their marriage. I suspected this was a psychological resistance that served to avoid dealing with the real issues at hand: the absence of intimacy and Joe's infidelity.

Lorna kept talking so I cut her off. She looked like she was going to snap. But I knew she wouldn't; it was indecent.

"Look, you two," I said, shifting eye contact between the two of them. "Two years. Every month for two years you have been coming here. And we have never addressed anything of substance. Lorna." I could see she was holding her breath, waiting for a barrage. "You talk for half an hour about some innocuous event. But this isn't Sunday tea. Joe, you sit there quietly, checking the clock, waiting for the session to end. As far as I'm concerned, you're both guilty of avoiding working on the reason you're here. And, frankly, so am I for letting this go on so long."

They were silent. The green banker's lamp on my desk hummed. The clock seemed to tick louder. I could hear them breathing, see their eyes flicking back and forth nervously. I could almost feel their hearts beating faster.

If I hadn't been so tired, I could have approached this less bluntly. But I was exhausted, my back was aching, so I had little time for bullshit. That little intervention would have caused analysts back at the institute to keel over on their overstuffed couches.

Lorna's hands balled up, squeezing the fabric of her dress. Joe shifted his legs so that his knees were now touching.

"So tell me now. Can we work on what you're here for? Can we stop wasting our time?"

"Joe's never home," Lorna said, conviction in her voice.

"She won't have sex," Joe countered.

"How is she supposed to have sex if you're never home?"

Lorna smiled and lowered her shoulders an inch. "Like last night, Joe left and didn't return until three in the morning."

Joe's eyes widened, as though he was shocked she was keeping track of him. No doubt he was out seeing Wanda last night, though I did my best to ignore this piece of knowledge.

"And why would he come home, Lorna, if he doesn't get any intimacy?"

Her head snapped back a few inches, like I had sucker-punched her. It was the first unrehearsed motion I'd seen in her since their therapy started.

Had I known Joe was having an affair with Wanda, I wouldn't have taken him and Lorna on as clients. But Wanda only disclosed her affair after I had started therapy with the Barringtons. It took a lot of compartmentalization on my part, but I was good at keeping secrets.

Joe and Lorna had come from very different upbringings. Joe was heir to the Bluebird Matchstick fortune. His family owned half of the marina, and he was the high school quarterback always destined for greatness. At least on a Bridgetown scale.

Lorna grew up in a mobile home outside of Bridgetown with devout evangelical parents who believed that any misbehavior was due to direct intervention by the devil.

Somehow the two of them got together and wanted a baby. Years of trying and nothing. Fertility tests showed no abnormalities. So, eventually, the sex just dried up.

Joe and Lorna stared at me, clutching the arms of the chairs, bracing themselves for the next blow.

There was a legendary story in psychotherapist circles of Milton Erickson. He was an eccentric and largely self-taught psychoanalyst from the Midwest who used unconventional methods in therapy. He combined hypnotic techniques, a firm knowledge of the human psyche, and good old country boy charm to become one of the most renowned mid-century psychiatrists. I was tired, and I felt disinhibited, so I conjured up some Milton.

"You two need shock therapy."

They both crinkled their noses.

"Shock therapy?" Joe said.

"Yeah. There's electroshock treatment, but then there's psychological shock treatment. That's the one you need."

"What are you talking about, Doc?"

"I need to know." I leaned forward, my hands pressed together in front of my face. "Do you want your relationship to improve?"

Both nodded.

"Are you willing to do what it takes?"

They nodded again, but hesitantly.

"Then shock therapy is what you need."

I could hear Lorna swallow. Joe snickered and looked away. But I had them intrigued.

"Do we have a deal?" I held out my hand to seal the deal.

Joe threw an arm up and came in for the handshake. I gripped his hand, and as we pulled back, I kept my thumb and little finger gently pressed against his hand. I brushed his palm with my middle finger. As I released, Joe's hand stayed in the air, waiting for the handshake to finish. I quickly took Lorna's hand and did the same.

They sat there staring at me, and I was able to hold their eyes in a moment of mild hypnosis.

"Deal?" I said.

Their hands dropped back onto their laps and they looked at me with uncertainty.

"Sorry, Doc, what?"

"Do we have a deal?" I said. "For the shock therapy."

Lorna nodded, and Joe followed.

"What I need you to do is go home." I took a deep breath, and for a moment I had a second thought about going through with it, but decided to press forward. "And fuck like animals."

Lorna gasped and Joe started laughing nervously. They exchanged glances. This was the first time I had seen them look at each other in session.

"I'm serious," I doubled down. "You rip her clothes off. You spank him. You both scream so loud the neighbors wonder if you're okay. Pull each other's hair. Whatever you're into."

Lorna was laughing a bit now. I was tapping into her underlying desires.

"Be the animals you are."

I smiled, and the two of them gazed at each other, their eyes filled with desire.

"That was very inappropriate," Lorna said, still smiling.

"Unexpected," Joe added.

"It's shock therapy. That's what it's supposed to do. I'll see you next week."

After they left, I sat there, hoping Lorna wouldn't report me to my licensing body for being a sexually deviant quack. I'd have a hell of a time explaining what just happened, but I felt that a mild hypnosis was necessary. Lorna had such inhibitions that a bomb was required to break that dam.

And it was urgent, because their marriage was hanging by a

thread. The two of them staying together was best for everyone. Including Wanda.

I was finishing the last few lines of my notes on the session with the Barringtons in their blue notebook, which was the shadow file. Each entry started on a new page, and the notes ranged anywhere from a few lines to a few pages. My colleagues had often criticized me for keeping bare-bones notes, but I wanted to record as little information as possible. I treated my notes as little jogs for my memory rather than a transcript. In the event that my notes were ever stolen, they would be close to unintelligible to anyone else. It helped ensure my patients' secrets were safe. But I had been keeping more details lately because of my patchy recollection.

A knock at the door. Sheila poked her head in.

"Sheriff Weagle is here to see you."

"He wants more therapy?"

After his sheepishness last night, I sensed that Ernie probably wanted to work something out. Therapy often went like that. Rather than a single episode, people required a few rounds of treatment before they got resolution.

"No, he said it was police business."

I put down my pen, thinking of the kettle and my episodes. Did Herman tell them about having to rescue me in the woods? The last thing I needed was for them to demand I take cognitive tests. A fire in a small town was always a big deal. The sheriffs normally spent their time catching drunk drivers and settling property disputes. An investigation into a fire could be the most exciting thing they did all year.

"Sure, let him in."

Ernie stepped inside, followed by Debbie Parks. They both

carried notepads. Ernie chewed gum. Debbie looked even more serious than usual. I shook their hands and invited them to sit down.

"Is my house okay to enter yet? To get my stuff?"

Debbie and Ernie looked at each other. Debbie said, "We don't know. We haven't been in touch with the firefighters."

"We can look into it," Ernie said.

"Do you need more information about the fire? I can try to go through what I remember ab-"

"Dr. Young, we're not here because of the fire," Debbie said. Her voice was sharp.

"No?"

"Wanda Flynn," Ernie said.

I grunted. I wouldn't acknowledge that I knew Wanda, but I wondered what kind of trouble she'd gotten herself into.

"A patient of yours."

"I can't tell you one way or the other. Confidentiality."

"We know she's a patient of yours."

I shrugged. I wouldn't let my body language betray my oath.

Ernie leaned forward, chewing his gum aggressively. "She was found in front of her home early this morning. Shot dead."

9

I shot up so fast I nearly tipped over my armchair. I put my hand on my forehead and paced behind Ernie and Debbie before steadying myself against the wall. The walls seemed to pulsate around me, and nausea bubbled in my gut. I blocked out everything around me.

Wanda lived on the edge, but not so close that anyone would want to kill her. And she was turning her life around. I immediately thought of her last visit. Wanda had been fearful of her brother, worried he might seek revenge. I reassured her that it was safe. I pressed and pressed her to resolve matters with him. She trusted me. And now she was dead.

"We're sorry, Gus," Ernie said.

I still didn't respond, partly because my oath of confidentiality lasted beyond the grave. Partly because I was still thinking about how a brother could bring himself to kill his sister.

"We need information from you." Debbie stood and walked over to me. "Her brother, Randy, was released from prison recently. She testified against him in his trial; it was the final nail. Did she ever talk about him?"

"Maybe you should find him."

"We already have him in custody," Ernie said, still sitting on the edge of his seat, his back to me. He was smacking his gum. "He says he has an alibi for last night; we're checking that out. So if he's innocent, we have an open case on our hands."

"Did Wanda ever say anything about anyone she was close to? Did she talk about anyone she was frightened of? I mean in her line of-"

"I'm not sure you two understand," I said, walking around the chairs so I could look at both Ernie and Debbie. "I keep confidential anything people talk about in here. That includes the identity of my clients. If one of you was a client of mine, I'm sure you wouldn't want me spilling your secrets."

Ernie stopped chewing.

"You do know that if we get a warrant," Debbie said, "you would have to hand over your case notes?"

Debbie was technically correct. By law, upon presentation of a warrant, I would be required to hand over my notebooks. This was the reason that I intentionally kept vague notes, using language that provided very little in the way of substantive information. If anyone ever got hold of Wanda's official record, they would conclude little except that Wanda was seeing me for relationship problems.

But the shadow files contained more details. These included my observations during sessions, links that I made between a client's present problems and their past relationships, and observations of my own feelings and reactions during sessions. It was sort of like a psychological diary. Courts have been inconsistent at best at forcing therapists to hand those documents over.

"That's fine," I said.

"Gus," Ernie said, making eye contact again. "We respect

what you do here, but there is a fairly good possibility that Randy, her brother, has an alibi that will check out."

"Which means that someone else shot her. Dr. Young, we don't just want your notes. We were wondering if we could enlist your help?"

I realized then why Ernie and Debbie had come to see me so quickly after Wanda's death. The victim's shrink isn't typically the first person that the sheriff visits in an investigation. I wanted to shut down right then and retreat to my cabin. But I also wanted to know if Randy killed Wanda.

"We know that you used to work big cases that included profiling work. We're a tiny detachment here, so if you could help, maybe make a profile of who could have done this, we'd have somewhere to start."

I had been a hired gun. In my last few years at the institute, while my star was still rising, ruthless defense attorneys enlisted me to help get their clients off or earn early releases. I was mired in debt at the time. I never lied, I never stretched the truth. But I was convincing and confident.

And I was wrong once.

"If you know that about me, then you know my track record is spotty."

"Even if you could come to the crime scene, see if you have any insights. It'll help us get whoever did this."

I nodded but didn't say anything. I wasn't sure I could be impartial on this one. I stared at the Barringtons' notebook on the side table.

Ernie rose and motioned for Debbie. "Think about it, Gus."

My eyes lingered on the coils of the blue notebook. Something Ernie had said prompted a memory.

"What time was she shot?"

"The best estimate is sometime before two a.m. Why?"

I looked down at the notebook. "No reason. Just wondering."

After they left and the door closed, I opened the Barrington's blue notebook to today's entry. I scanned the page, stopping at something Lorna had said.

Last night Joe left and didn't return until three in the morning.

I drove southwest out of Bridgetown, into Maine's wooded interior and toward Wanda's house along the 112. Somehow managed to get myself turned around, so to save time I decided to cut through an old logging road. White pine, red spruce, and birch formed a corridor along the washed-out gravel road filled with deep mud puddles. The rain had turned to mist, but droplets still clung to branches like honey. The sun was trying to break through the blanket of clouds that hung low over the treetops. Black bears and moose lived here and were foraging this time of year, using these old roads as thruways. This was the area where I'd spent my childhood summers. Every August the institute shut down and the other analysts headed to Cape Cod or the Hamptons. My mother would load up our blue Ford Galaxie and drive up to Harmony, population nine hundred and thirty-six, where she had grown up.

I came to Bridgetown mainly for nostalgia and to escape. My mother had developed Alzheimer's three years ago and insisted on being put in a home near Harmony, so in Bridgetown I was close to her in case she needed anything, but my visits were few and far between.

My truck lurched over the holes and bumps in the road, dug out by logging trucks driving over soft dirt. Rocks rang off the wheel well as the truck swayed back and forth.

Wanda said that she planned to go public with Joe's affair after his no-show at the bar. She was a loose cannon, but she had also developed the ability to calm herself quickly. So I would be surprised if she really did go through with it. But even so, I couldn't see Joe shooting her point blank.

Joe looked rested in session. No bags under his eyes, clean-shaven, no added tension in his face. Joe was a narcissist, but only a true psychopath could kill his mistress and eight hours later show up to marriage counseling like nothing happened.

Wanda was a project of mine. The world was stacked against her. She was given no chance in life, but she had a spirit that I felt I could unleash if given enough time. Maybe that was my own issue: I wanted to be her savior.

I had no sexual desire toward Wanda, but I had an affinity for her beyond what I had for most clients. I needed to see her overcome her demons.

Up ahead, three fallen fir trees blocked the road. I stopped the truck and tried to lift one, but like a vise around my waist, my back tightened before I managed to drag it an inch. My shortcut wouldn't pan out. I got back in the truck, five-point turned on the narrow path, and headed back to the highway.

A phone call came through on Bluetooth.

"Good morning," Renee said when I answered. "How was the hotel?"

It was good to hear her voice, temporarily making me forget about Wanda.

"Lumpy mattress, stale coffee, scratchy towels."

"Lovely," she said as my truck bottomed out over a boulder the size of a basketball. "Your kitchen is out of commission for a while. So I was thinking maybe I could take you out for dinner?"

I was approaching the highway. A sheriff's cruiser was parked at the intersection, blocking the path.

"I'd love that," I said, nearing the cruiser. "I've got to go, but how about I pick you up at seven?"

"It's a date."

I stopped and threw my truck in park, but left it running as I slowly got out. Light rain was still falling. I approached the cruiser's passenger side. The window rolled down, and Debbie Parks leaned over from behind the wheel.

"Lost, Doctor?"

"I was, um, just trying to cut across this old road. To get there."

"To the Flynn trailer?"

I nodded.

"The home is over that way." She pointed with her thumb in the opposite direction. She seemed to be looking for a reaction, but I didn't take the bait. Then she offered, "It's easy to get turned around back here. Come on, follow me. I'll get you there."

I tailed Debbie's cruiser down two empty single-lane highways lined by thick woods and broken by gray lakes. The only signs of civilization were mailboxes spaced miles apart. They stood at the edges of driveways that weaved through the forest into cabins hidden from view.

I saw the blue and red lights ahead. Three cruisers and an ambulance were lined up, blocking the road. One officer patrolled the perimeter while three others wearing rubber gloves milled around Wanda's property. Paramedics waited beside the ambulance. Behind the cruisers, yellow police tape cordoned off the highway between the drainage ditches. A white sheet covered a body in the middle of the road. A medical examiner in a white jumpsuit and booties knelt down and placed yellow numbered markers beside the body.

Wanda's trailer was more run-down than when I had last driven past. Last summer, after she had no-showed for two appointments in a row, I decided to drive by her place to check on her. She was hunched over, pulling weeds from her flower garden filled with peonies, gladiolas, and daisies. She didn't notice me, and I was satisfied she was safe, so I drove away.

The streaks of algae that clung to the white vinyl siding begged for a pressure wash. One of the teal window shutters hung by a single screw. The rusty storm door wasn't fully shut and creaked as the wind whipped it back and forth. She kept pots of wilted fall mums around the edges of the trailer.

Ernie Weagle stood on Wanda's driveway, his back turned to me as he spoke to a man. I got out of my truck and followed Debbie. As we approached them, I saw that the other man was Night Hawk Ned.

"No," Ned said. "I said it was 5:15. Still dark and looked like someone clobbered a deer. And someone has been. This month alone, I scraped off six. Two six-point bucks. Someone's mowing them down, I tell you-"

"Ned," Ernie said calmly. "Can we stick to what you found at 5:15 a.m.?"

"That whistleblowing whore." Ned pointed at me. "He knows her. She goes to his back room at Buck's."

"You found Ms. Flynn."

"Yup. I rolled her over, was gonna start CPR. I was actually the person who came up with thirty pumps, two breaths. Red Cross stole it from me, 'cause they saw me one day down by the beach pulling this young girl from a rip tide. Next thing you know it's nationwide. Worldwide. And nothing for me. I've sent them a hundred cease and desist-"

"Did you see anyone else? Any cars, bikes, people, anything?"

"She's got men coming in and outta here. A big conveyor belt of-"

"Last night, Ned. Last night."

"I find her, see she's dead. I call you and then it took FORTY-FIVE minutes for you to come. I could've been dead if the killer was still there."

Ernie rubbed his forehead. I sympathized with his struggle to rein Ned in enough to get a coherent statement.

"Debbie," Ernie said, "could you take Ned and get a written statement?"

Debbie raised her eyebrows and muttered as she walked past Ernie, "You're lucky you outrank me."

Ned kept talking as Debbie led him to her cruiser.

"We could use your help, Gus," Ernie said. "I think Randy's alibi will turn out solid and then we'll have no leads. I know you've moved past the forensic stuff and I don't blame you after what happened."

"I can't give up clinical information. You of all people know how important it is that I keep things hidden."

"But even if you don't tell us anything clinical, could you give us some ideas. Maybe from statements. The body?"

The thought of seeing Wanda dead turned my stomach. My goal had always been to help her live a full life and thrive. That was ripped away. I decided I needed to see her. I needed to break through denial and know that she was gone. I would channel the anger to find her killer.

"Okay. I'll help. Limited, though."

"Let's start with the body."

I followed Ernie under the police tape toward the white sheet. The medical examiner, a woman in her mid-thirties with blonde hair and wide eyes, stood up as we approached.

"Could we have a look?" Ernie said. "And a rundown."

She slowly pulled the sheet back. I felt blood rush up to my face. I regretted agreeing to see the body. The picture of Wanda as the witty, fiery yet soft-hearted woman would be stained by Wanda the corpse. She lay face down on the asphalt, wearing jeans and a white tank top stained dark red. Her legs were splayed wide, one hand by her side, the other awkwardly over her head. Her hair was messy, stained red from the gaping hole in the back of her skull. Through her hair, I could see part of her face turned to the left on the pavement, mouth open. She looked plastic, like a big Barbie scribbled with red Sharpie.

I took two steps back and turned from Wanda as the medical examiner began speaking.

"Two shots, one to the back of the head, no exit wound. The second in the middle of her back, exiting through her sternum. Likely severed her vertebrae. Likely died instantly."

At least she didn't suffer. I could see the eulogy cliché already. But she suffered. Her life was one big exercise in suffering.

"Bullet?" Ernie said.

"Actually, I recovered a casing from the ditch." She held it up.

Ernie snapped on a rubber glove and examined it.

"Is this, what, a thirty-three?"

She shook her head. "Nope. It's a .303."

Ernie raised his eyebrows. "Not a lot of guns fire a .303."

"Exactly. We're running a check."

I took a deep breath and tried to appear calm as they examined the casing, but my heart felt like it was in my shoes. The Lee-Enfield No.4 I own uses 0.303-diameter bullets.

10

My heart pounded like a fugitive on the run as I tore up the old highway to my cabin. The sun was dipping below the tree line, shining right in my eyes, so I could barely see the road. Luckily, there were no cars in either lane. No one traveled back here. Not unless they had to.

My father left behind the Lee-Enfield No. 4 after he'd taken off. A grandfather I had never met used it in World War II. It was the oldest gun I owned. I had only shot it a half dozen times, but kept it as the only connection I had to my absentee dad and my British roots.

In hindsight, the sheriff inviting me to the crime scene was unusual. After years as a forensic psychoanalyst, no one had ever asked me to visit a scene. Debbie seemed suspicious of my every move, making me wonder whether they brought me to Wanda's house to show me the casing and see my reaction.

It didn't mean that Wanda was shot by my gun. Other guns fire .303-diameter bullets. It was nothing but a coincidence that she was shot dead by a rare bullet used in one of the guns I own. Maine is full of gun enthusiasts. Over half of adults in the state own them, and aren't required to register them. I never bothered to either.

Someone wanted her dead. They used a gun with a long range. Perhaps they didn't want to get close to her.

I thought about possible suspects. Joe Barrington. Wanda threatened to tell Lorna about their affair. But would Joe really kill her for that, and then show up at couples therapy like nothing happened?

Buddy pimped Wanda. He would be motivated to protect her. Did she owe him money? Leaving the business to be with Joe once and for all would mean Buddy would lose an important source of revenue.

I thought of Randy, her little brother, the jailbird. He'd killed before and Wanda helped put him away. The parole board thought he was rehabilitated. A low risk to re-offend. He said he found Jesus. Hallelujah.

Wanda was a hooker. She had enemies. Maybe a sadistic John passed through town and decided to satisfy all his primal urges. And he just happened to use a gun with 0.303 bullets.

I'd been in the Comfort Inn all night. The boys hockey team. Their feet stomping up and down the hall all night, running back, giggling. The ice machine dumping ice. I remembered that. I wasn't losing time. I was just a bit absentminded. I wouldn't forget shooting someone.

Sheila saw me in the morning. She woke me up. I was dirty and she wanted me to shower. No blood on me. I took a shallow breath and exhaled. I reminded myself that I was innocent.

I pulled up my driveway and looked at my half-charred home. Contractors must have stopped by and boarded up the windows in the addition. Soot streaked up the siding toward the roof. The inspectors hadn't cleared the house yet, but I needed to get inside.

The cabin's old entrance was a sliding patio door off the

wraparound deck that led to the kitchen. I pulled the door open and stepped inside. The power was still cut, so I grabbed the LED lantern off the fridge, flicked it on, and made my way to the basement.

Cold white light spread across the basement. High file cabinets lined three walls, half full of yellow notebooks, the rest containing the blue notebook shadow files from patients I had seen over the decades. My work bench and power tools sat along the fourth wall. Next to the table saw was the gun locker. I didn't touch the combination. Since my memory problems surfaced, I kept the door closed but unlocked.

I closed my eyes and reminded myself of the five guns I still owned. A Remington 7600 pump action, a Model Seven Bolt action, the BAR lightweight wood model with the twenty-inch barrel, a savage 99, and the Lee. I also kept a Sig Sauer in my office safe.

I opened my eyes slowly and raised the lantern. I had to force myself to look inside the gun locker. My eyes drifted from firearm to firearm, reluctant to look at the slot where I remembered placing the Lee-Enfield. Four weapons stood where I remembered them. The fifth was empty.

That was where I'd left the Lee, I was certain, though I hadn't used it in ages. Last spring, I considered selling it at a gun fair in New Hampshire but never went through with it. Part of me still wanted to keep my father's memory.

I tried to avoid thinking about what it all meant, but I couldn't resist. There had to be an explanation. Someone stole the gun and used it to kill Wanda.

Or Wanda's killer happened to have a weapon that fired the same caliber round. And the gun was missing because I had sold the Lee a few years ago and it slipped my mind.

Or.

I put the lantern down and steadied myself against the cabinet, feeling like I was going to dry heave. A fog descended over me, leaving me frozen in place. I couldn't let the sheriff know about the missing gun. Unless he already did.

It wasn't registered, so it couldn't be traced back to me and was no longer in my possession. The sheriff's department didn't have it, at least as far as I knew. I thought about reporting my gun stolen, but voluntarily divulging the information wouldn't spare me any grief. Whoever killed Wanda either still had it or had ditched it somewhere.

If the gun was recovered and was in fact mine, I could plead ignorance. I could say I hadn't realized it was missing.

I ran my hands through my hair, telling myself I wasn't crazy. The gun couldn't be traced to me, but police could trace the cartridge's lot number. I had to get rid of the remaining rounds.

I knelt down and put the lantern on the floor in front of the locker, then pulled boxes of rounds off the bottom shelf, looking for the .303s. I had ordered a box a year ago but never used it. I found it, and before I opened it I could feel the cartridges rolling around the box. I flipped the lid open. Four rounds were missing.

I felt a buzz in my pocket and pulled out my phone. Unknown caller.

Without thinking, I swiped.

"Hello?"

"Hi, Dad."

My racing heart felt like it stopped altogether. I'd resigned myself to never hearing from my estranged daughter again.

"Karen?" The word came out like a gasp.

"Hi."

"Oh my God, I..." I shut the cabinet and paced back and forth. "I'm so happy you called."

There was static on the phone. She was exhaling. I turned to head upstairs, but in doing so I inadvertently kicked the box of rounds over, sending them rolling all over the dark basement. I crouched down, holding the phone to my ear, searching for the cartridges.

"Sorry," Karen said.

I stood up. My back seized and I tried to press on my hip to ease some of the pressure. "No, no. You don't be sorry, Karen. Me. I am."

A long pause. My half-baked apology hung in the air. It was insufficient, but it was a start. She didn't acknowledge the apology, but she didn't hang up either.

"I've only got a few minutes right now. But... I got the letter you sent and I'm going to be passing through. Work trip. Maybe we can meet? Coffee or something?"

The envelope. I wished that Karen were calling because of something other than a pile of cash. But this was a start. "Yes. Maybe even, even-" I thought of my burnt house. If the electricity was turned back on, the kitchen would be functional. "If you came for dinner?"

"I'd like that."

"When will you be here?"

"In two days."

A dog barked outside and footsteps crunched on the gravel. "Can I pick you up?"

"I'll get myself there."

"Do you need directions? It's pretty remote."

"Everything's on Google now. Even you. How's seven?"

"Yes."

The phone clicked off and I briefly forgot about Wanda and the gun. I reminded myself that the gun must have been stolen because I had left the cabinet unlocked. But if anyone asked, I never realized my gun was missing, so I couldn't report it. That was my story.

But a stolen gun could help the investigation into Wanda's death. The sheriffs asked me to join their investigation, so I could reveal that my gun was stolen at my discretion.

I climbed up the stairs from the basement and looked out the patio window. Herman stood holding an old kerosene lantern in one hand and Anna on a leash in the other.

Anna burst inside, and when I knelt down she jumped all over me. "Thanks for watching Anna, Herman."

"They let you back in?"

"No electricity, not yet. But I figure I can at least sleep in my bed."

"Still smells bad." He took a little swig from his flask. "Want to come over for dinner?"

"Shit." I looked at my watch. I remembered I had made plans for dinner with Renee. "I'm supposed to meet someone in town."

"That dead-eyed daisy, eh?"

"Excuse me?"

Herman raised his hand and walked away. "Don't mind me none. Just an out-of-date ol' drunk."

"You said something about a daisy?"

Herman turned. "I said she's got dead eyes. Just watch yourself. You're a doc. Women can smell money."

I shook my head. Herman didn't trust anyone either. He'd been living the hermit life for almost twenty years. I'd heard a rumor that he was a suspect in a missing person's case back in the eighties before he retreated out here. I looked at him and for a moment I thought I saw my future.

Herman winked. "She's prob'ly a maniac in the sack, though."

11

Small towns on the Eastern seaboard usually have three types of restaurants. There's the seaside, rural-upscale establishment, which usually means old carpet and dim lights with tacky nautical accents overlooking a fisherman's wharf where deep-fried foods are served. There's the national chain that decided to roll the dice and try their luck with a franchisee in a town of ten thousand people. They also served fried food. Then there's the greasy spoon, where tables and seats are easily wipeable but not always wiped, and locals come for the daily specials. And the deep fry.

The Oarhouse Diner fell into the third category. The special was a four-dollar club sandwich with curly fries and coleslaw in a Dixie cup. The building was a former brothel, converted some twenty years ago. The diner's owner, Karl Svetburg, decided on the name "Oarhouse" to pay tribute to the building's roots, with all the subtlety you'd expect from a part-time trucker and full-time alcoholic. I thought the name was charming.

Before leaving my cabin I decided that I had to upgrade from my hunting jacket and camo pants if I wanted to make an impression with Renee. I found the best clean clothes in my closet and changed into a light denim shirt, tucked into my faded Wranglers, and my old black cowboy boots. I decided against my desert suede jacket in case the fringes turned Renee off.

I parked in front of the diner, flipped down the sun visor, and gave myself a once-over in the mirror. I ran my fingers through my beard to smooth it out and swept my hair back. It was as long as I'd ever worn it, not quite long enough to tie back but enough that I could tuck it behind my ears.

When I opened the door, the bell hanging over it announced my presence. The vinyl stools along the bar were empty, but half of the booths were full. Dolly Parton classics played on the radio, and low chatter hummed throughout the diner. I wondered whether they were talking about Wanda's murder. News like that would spread through town like a virus during a pandemic. I could smell coffee and fried lard. Lard made everything taste better.

I saw a few familiar faces, but they were buried in plates of fish and chips or chowders. Rosemary Grandin, one of Sheila's closest friends and a prolific cross-stitcher, looked up from her garden salad and waved. I could sense her eyes tracking me as I made my way to the back of the diner. I hoped to keep my date secret from Sheila, but I knew enough about Rosemary to realize that she would call her to gossip about Renee before I had a chance to order.

"Gus." Renee was sitting in the corner booth, waving me over. Her eyes lit up when she saw me. She wore a navy T-shirt with a black blazer, and had a colorful scarf wrapped around her neck. Her hair was pulled back and held with a wood clip.

She stood up and put her arms around me. I pulled her close and she rested her cheek on my shoulder. I could smell citrus in her hair.

"You poor thing." She pulled back and let her hand fall into mine. "What a day you've had. Let me order you something strong."

I thought about going straight for the double bourbon my circumstances called for, but decided I needed to keep a level head.

"It's okay. Maybe just coffee."

I sat down on the side of the booth facing the entrance. An old habit, but it made me comfortable. While training as an intern on an inpatient psychiatric unit, a patient put me in a chokehold because I refused to give him a weekend pass home. It took three orderlies to pull him off me, and he ended up staying in the quiet room for three days.

Renee slid into the seat across from me and took a sip from the glass of house white sitting in front of her.

"I'm sorry about Wanda," she said.

I gave the standard shrink "Hmmm." I couldn't acknowledge or deny that I knew Wanda.

"Losing a patient, especially like this, it must be-" She drifted off, twirling the jam holder. "I know she was your patient, Gus. I fill her prescriptions."

My mind drifted to the rounds scattered along the basement floor. I couldn't forget to find and dispose of them.

"How do you deal with it?"

I felt a heaviness in my chest. Renee had these saucer-like eyes, inviting me in. The idea that someone cared about how I felt was irresistible.

"The truth is, I don't know if I've been coping all that well lately."

The waitress came by to pass us the laminated menus and pour me some coffee. She walked a couple of steps away before I called her back. I'd just lost a patient and may have been the owner of the murder weapon. Some situations called for sober minds. Others for forty proof.

"Could I have a bourbon and Coke too?" I said. "Double."

Renee smiled, unable to hold back a playful snicker.

"I can't talk to you about patients, Renee. It's a promise I make to them. I take what they tell me to the grave."

"Is that hard? Keeping all that in?"

"It's the only way."

"Only way what?"

"That I can help people. They need to be able to speak freely. Whether it's hard for me doesn't matter."

I left out the part that lately it seemed like I couldn't remember half of what people told me anyway.

"Noble."

I couldn't tell if that was a dig or sign of admiration. Not everyone agreed with me. Alistair had criticized me for applying confidentiality too rigidly. "There's a moral obligation to the patient, Gus. But there's also a moral obligation to everyone else. Sometimes, flexibility is required." What Alistair didn't understand was that the patient was the only point of therapeutic intervention. I had the ability and skills to help the patient, to change them, and no one else. I would never stop believing that people could make meaningful changes in their lives.

I had the power to fix the patient, but I couldn't fix society. If I betrayed my patient's confidence, therapy was effectively over and I could no longer fix their problem. Then society would be at risk. And so would the patient. It was a lose-lose.

Renee twirled a strand of hair around her finger.

"Sorry, I just find it fascinating. What must be held up there." She pointed at her forehead.

"It's not as interesting as you'd think."

"I'm sure it is." She smiled. "But I like mysterious guys. But you dealt with this all the time before. Murderers."

"What do you mean?"

"I looked you up, remember? You can't hide anymore. You did all those big forensic cases."

"That was another lifetime."

"What was it like? Staring down a psychopath."

I thought back to those years when I was at the top of my game, seeing one court-ordered assessment after another. I felt like I could take on any case. I never felt out of my depth. Part of me wanted to be that person again.

"Well, as a psychiatrist, it's not too difficult because I can figure out their M.O. pretty quickly."

"What is it?"

"Well, a psychopath just wants to get one over on you. In any way possible. They thrive on owning people. Controlling them. It's power."

"How do they do that?"

Renee cradled her wine glass and leaned forward, lips parted. I had her captivated.

"They have a radar for detecting people's vulnerabilities. They home in and just manipulate the shit out of it. Life's a game to them."

"Sounds like my ex-husband." She laughed. "So how do you deal with them?"

"You have to catch them as they are doing the con and show them you're not scared. Call them on it. And if you can, figure out their vulnerability and make sure they know you know it."

"So interesting," Renee said. "You can do that? Figure it out?"

"Sometimes."

"Okay then, Doctor." She bit her lower lip. "What's my vulnerability?"

It had been so long since a woman took such an interest in me. Warmth filled my face. I took her hand.

"Well, you moved to a small town, you have a crazy ex-husband, you're interested in my secrets but give very little of your own. You're joyful and bubbly most of the time, but that belies something underneath. I suspect you're relieved you're here, away from where you were, and you're more comfortable talking about others than thinking about your own life. So there's something in your past, a wound, a loss, something that you avoid. It still hurts."

Renee pulled her hand back and her eyes changed, as though I'd poked through her facade too hard.

"I'm sorry," I said. "I don't know anything about you."

For a moment I thought she might cry. Instead she sat back and nodded, looking impressed by my formulation.

"You're good." She smiled. "Enough about me. What's your vulnerability?"

I swept my hair to the side and leaned forward. "I'd have to say beautiful women. A witty sense of humor. Blondes."

"Oh boy," she said, jokingly pulling at her collar. "You're laying it on thick."

"Is it working?"

I was half done with my club and deep into my third double bourbon when I saw Joe Barrington walk into the diner. His white dress shirt collar was open wide, a thick gold chain visible across the top of his chest. He swung his arms and took long, confident strides. He stopped at a few tables to shake the hands of some townsfolk, giving others a pat on the back and a wink.

He was with three other men. I recognized one as Chris Forbes, Joe's brother-in-law and Lorna's brother. He was a portly man, and his skinny legs and the red plaid shirt stretched over his round belly made him look like a walking candy apple. Chris owned three of the car dealerships that hugged the highway into Bridgetown. I didn't recognize the other two men.

Renee was midway into a story about summers she spent at her cottage during her childhood. But I drifted off as Joe and his companions sat down at a booth on the other side of the diner.

Renee kept talking as I tried to discreetly look past her, over her shoulder. Joe sat laughing, drinking, leaning back in the booth with his arm draped over the top of the backrest. Like nothing happened.

The woman he had an affair with for years was dead. The woman he was going to leave his wife for was lying face down on cold pavement, shot in the head.

And yet he was here, carrying on with the boys.

The booze had me feeling pretty good.

"Renee, you'll have to excuse me."

I got up, wiped my mouth with the napkin, and headed over to Joe's table. He sat against the window, wedged in the booth beside Chris Forbes. He was telling some story about the last time he was at the driving range and pinged one off the ball picker. The bastard was so enthralled by his story, he didn't notice me until the others turned their heads to stare. Joe looked up. His mouth dropped open half an inch.

"Mr. Mayor." I put my hand on the table to keep from swaying. "I need to talk to you."

"Sorry, but I'm busy-"

"It can't wait."

"Look, maybe we can set something up for tomorrow." He reached into his pocket and pulled out a business card.

"Right fucking now."

"Whoa, whoa," Chris Forbes said, raising his meaty hands, motioning for me to take things down a notch. His face turned red, and his neck veins popped up. I wondered if Chris knew that Joe was nailing Wanda behind his sister's back.

"It's okay, Chris." Joe flicked at his mustache a few times. "It's okay."

Chris shimmied out of the booth to let Joe out, then stood two inches from my face. I didn't step back and kept eye contact. I wasn't about to let him intimidate me.

Joe motioned to an empty booth in the corner of the diner. As I followed him there, he glared at me over his shoulder.

"What the hell?" Joe whispered as he slid into the booth.

"I could say the same to you."

"Doc, you're drunk. I can smell it on you."

"Wanda Flynn was found murdered today."

I stared at Joe. He looked out the window and rolled his necklace between his fingers.

"What do you want me to do, Doc?"

"Maybe show some respect?"

"I'm sad, okay? Really sad. But my relationship with her was a secret. And it has to stay that way."

He hung his head and looked up at me with reddened eyes. I gave little back.

"It has to stay that way." His voice rose. "Right? Your little spiel about confidentiality and all that?"

"You had reason to." The bourbon was full force now. I realized I was walking a fine line between confronting Joe and breaching my oath.

"Listen, you fucking piece of shit." Joe leaned over the table but lowered his voice. "You've already crossed the line. You push it further and I out you."

"Go ahead, tell the licensing body that I confronted you in a diner." My words were slurred, slipping out of my mouth. "You bring it out and you become a suspect in a murder investigation."

"I didn't do anything. I loved her. Let's make that clear. But I can go to your college and have them look into why you're meeting Buddy Getson in parking lots."

My mouth went dry.

"That's right. I know about that. So keep your promises, asshole."

―――――――――

After Joe returned to his table, I staggered toward my booth, but stopped at the counter and asked the waitress for one last bourbon. I pulled out my credit card to pay for my tab, but it slipped out of my hand and fell between the bar stools. As I knelt to clumsily search for it, I caught an elderly couple looking at me, their faces crinkled, slowly shaking their heads.

By the time I found the credit card and slid onto the stool, the waitress had already poured some Jim Beam over two big ice cubes. I had just put the glass to my mouth when I felt a hand on my shoulder.

I turned. Renee was already wearing her coat. I lifted my arms, moving in for a hug. She jerked out of the way and put a firm hand on my chest.

"You're going to need a drive home."

I raised the glass, but she touched my wrist and guided my hand down.

"Okay."

I signed for my tab and stuffed the receipt in my pocket. Renee walked behind me as I swayed back and forth, bumping into an empty booth and nearly losing my balance. She guided me forward, and I spilled out the door and fell onto the pavement. She grabbed my elbow and yanked me to my feet.

"You can drive my car." I fumbled the keys out of my pocket.

"No, we can take mine."

We got to her blue Golf, and I collapsed onto the passenger seat. I dropped the backrest so that I was leaning back, and everything started to spin slowly. Renee turned the ignition and we hit the road.

I was aware of what an ass I was making of myself on our first date. But she didn't leave me in the diner like I deserved either. That might have meant something. She was a decent person.

Meg wouldn't have stuck around through this sort of public embarrassment. At my last holiday party at the institute, while my personal and professional lives were unraveling, I decided to get systematically drunk. Halfway through my third double scotch, I realized she had left without saying a word, taking the car with her. I had to hitch an uncomfortable ride home with Alistair. When he dropped me off and I stumbled inside, I realized she wasn't there. She had inadvertently synced her phone with the computer, and when I sat down I saw the messages. Perhaps if I hadn't gotten drunk that night our relationship could have been salvaged. I still wondered if she meant for me to see those texts. Like little cuts in our emotional razor fight.

"I'm sorry about this."

"I can't blame you. Your house burns down, your patient gets killed," she said. "Just don't puke. I hate the smell."

"I'll try." I turned toward the window and rolled it down. The cold air hit my face. "Almost. My house almost burned down."

It took twenty minutes through dark roads to reach my place. During the drive I told her about seeing Wanda's body, the gunshots, and the casing. Even in my half-drunk stupor, I left out any clinical information. Renee didn't seem interested in knowing anything about Wanda anyway.

She parked in front of my cabin and then helped me to the patio door. The door was locked, so I asked her to go around the side and get the spare key from underneath a paving stone. We went inside, and she grabbed the lantern. I stopped in the kitchen and threw back three glasses of water along with the pills for my back.

Then I took off my shoes, flopped down on the bed, and crawled underneath the covers.

"I guess this was one way to get you into my bedroom," I said.

"Sorry, Gus, I'm just getting you home safe," Renee said. "This isn't how I envision this going."

I was stunned. Renee seemed so distant. Normally she would have made some sort of witty comment.

"I embarrassed you."

"No." She winced. "I think you embarrassed yourself. And pissed off the town mayor."

"I thought I was being discreet."

She shook her head. "The whole diner was looking at you."

I slid my leg over the edge of the bed and put my foot on the ground, an old trick I learned to help stop the spins.

"For what it's worth, Gus, he does seem like a jerk."

"Yeah."

Renee sat on the edge of the bed, staring out the window.

"Have I ruined my chance at a second date?"

She hesitated.

"My ex. He had a drinking problem. He was more dangerous, though."

"I don't normally do this."

"I gather that. Six drinks don't normally incapacitate people."

I smiled.

"Sorry to put you through that."

"I lost a lot because of it. Just brings up bad memories."

Even though I was almost unconscious, I felt guilty.

"But I understand how given your circumstances this would happen today."

"You know what is bothering me most about it?"

"What?"

"I have this feeling that somehow, whoever did this, is doing it to hurt me."

"What do you mean?"

"That Wanda was a casualty. That someone wanted to get at me, so they killed her. That-"

"That's drunk talk."

"Maybe I could have stopped it."

She touched my leg. "You feel guilty, Gus. You blame yourself. The truth is, there was nothing you could do to save her. You don't always have control."

She stood up to leave, running her hand against the door as she looked back at me.

"Can I see you again?" I asked. "I won't drink."

"Sure."

"Tomorrow evening?"

"Consider it a date."

12

"She had this hair, thick and beautiful. But if you ever tried to brush it"—Doug smiled longingly—"there was hell to pay. That little girl, hair all knotted and twisted. She had spirit. She had spunk."

Doug rubbed his hand over his heart as he reminisced about his daughter, Maddie. With his other hand he ran his fingers up and down the brass chain of the antique floor lamp beside him. It cast a dancing shadow against the wall. I offered an occasional grunt or nod, but my mind was elsewhere.

Maybe because I was hungover, my head woody and throbbing.

Renee didn't want to stay the night, probably because she was disgusted by my drunkenness. When I woke up and went to the kitchen to boil water for my morning coffee, part of me wished that Renee would be there. That she decided to stay the night to make sure I was safe. I hoped that she would see me again. Instead of calling her for a ride, I had to ask Sheila to pick me up.

As Doug continued to talk, I ran through my confrontation with Joe. I shouldn't have done that, especially in public. After my stunt in the diner, the whole town would soon know that I accused Joe of killing Wanda. But Joe wasn't a killer. He was simply a narcissist. I came close to breaking my oath, though, and that wasn't okay.

The first time Wanda came to a session, she was made up with cherry-red lipstick, foundation thick like it was painted on with a roller, tight jeans, and a low-cut T-shirt. She tested me, wanting to see if she could trust me or if I would see her as a sexual object, the way she saw herself.

It's true that I found her physically attractive. That was just a fact. But below that exterior existed a beautiful woman, one who was waiting to bloom. That's who I saw.

I loved Wanda. Not in a sexual way, but in the way a father loves his daughter. I cared about her growth as a person, and I was able to witness it happen.

And now it was all over. Before she ever had a chance to really live.

On my way to work, Debbie Parks had called to say that Wanda's brother Randy was no longer a suspect. He was at a Narcotics Anonymous meeting in Liverpool and went for a late coffee with one of the members afterward. He was dropped off at his apartment in Bridgetown at 1:30 a.m. Wanda's house was at least an hour walk from his place and he had no vehicle. He'd met with Wanda earlier that day at her place and she had dropped him off.

If this was true, I hadn't sent Wanda to her death. When Debbie told me that, I felt temporarily relieved. But there was still a possibility he made his way to her home. He had motive. And he'd killed before.

Doug stopped talking and was staring at me.

"She was yours, wasn't she?"

"Excuse me?"

"The murdered lady? She was your patient."

I sighed. Doug had noticed that I wasn't paying attention.

"Doug, as you know, I can't-"

"Yeah, I got it. You can't tell me nothing about others."

"Right."

Doug crossed his legs and leaned back in the chair. "What's it like for you, losing someone?"

"Doug, we're here for-"

"Yeah, but you're here, I'm talking about Maddie, and you're dealing with your shit. So let's sort that out. How do you do it?"

I was initially annoyed that Doug was calling me out on my lack of attention to him. But he was right, so I considered his question. He was a man feeling alone in his grief. Maybe it would help him to know that I get affected by loss too. That he's not the only one.

"It hurts. It hurts a lot when I lose people. I wonder if I could have done anything differently."

"Amen, brother. And 'cause of your job you must have to keep all of those regrets inside. You've just gotta hold it in."

People always wanted to know what secrets I kept, but even more about how I managed to keep them to myself. They thought I was a balloon full of confidential information just waiting to burst. But in truth, I was never as interested in the secrets as much as the person's reason for having them.

Your son was fathered by a seventy-year-old priest and your husband doesn't know? I want to know who you're protecting with your silence. Had an affair, the woman became pregnant, and you forced her to abort the fetus? I'd want to know who you envision judging you if it ever got out. That's the material we work on in therapy. It's not the action, it's the reasons behind the action that matter.

"It's not hard."

"It's not?"

I shook my head.

"Well, you've been wrestling with something for the past forty-five minutes."

Doug was angry with me. While I knew he was partly justified in his annoyance, I sensed that this was hitting a deeper nerve. Someone in his past must not have listened to him. I decided I had to turn things back around on Doug to find out.

"You feel like I've wasted your time today."

"Nah, I'm good. I'm good."

Doug stood up and made for the door.

"You don't feel like you can explore that with me."

"What?"

"Doug, on the one hand you're right. I wasn't paying full attention to you. But on the other hand, I'd like to work through it and see if we can move past it, figure out what it all means for you. And then you run for the door."

Doug crossed his arms. "You take care of yourself, Doc. I'll see you next time."

"Doug, please."

"Just one thing. Hopefully the police are looking at her brother. I wouldn't trust the guy."

He walked past me, knocking into my forearm as he left. Before I could ask Doug what he meant, he was already gone. I tried to rub the throbbing out of my temples. One thing Doug said was certainly correct: I had to take care of myself and was in no shape to be seeing clients today.

There was a soft knock at the door. Sheila poked her head in. Before she could speak, I cut her off.

"Sheila, I'm sorry to do this to you, but I've got to cancel the day. My head's not in it."

Her face tightened.

"What is it?"

"Well, Ned's here. And he's all over the map. He really wants to talk to you."

I had wondered if Wanda's murder would discombobulate Ned. He grew up in a backwoods compound with his father. From a young age, Ned had been digging out bunkers with his dad and setting up booby traps on the trails that crossed their land. They had weekly drills to prepare for a nuclear war.

When he was seven, Ned discovered his father dead of a self-inflicted gunshot to the head. He cleaned up the mess himself, didn't call the cops. His father had taught him not to trust authorities. It wasn't until a neighbor caught the smell weeks later that anyone knew what was going on.

Ned never shared that with me. Sheila told me. It was part of town lore.

"Sure. Send him in, but cancel the rest."

Ned opened the door a crack and slid in, his back to the wall. The smell of cigarettes wafted in with him. I took one look at him and knew things weren't going well. He had a ball cap pulled low, partly covering his eyes, and a hood tight over his head. He wore wraparound sunglasses even though the room was dim. His sweater covered his arms, and he wore gloves. Aside from his mouth and nose, no skin was exposed.

Ned made his way over to the chair, sat on the edge, and leaned forward. He pulled the hood back and took off his hat, revealing a shaved head. Ned had been proud of his long white mullet. He considered it his distinctive look.

"Ned, your hair."

He got up and dragged the floor fan between us, then turned it up to the maximum setting before speaking.

"I've gotta hide," he whispered. His eyebrows knitted together over his sunglasses. "They might be listening."

"Who?"

"They're following me."

"Who, Ned?"

He shook his head. "Can't tell you. I haven't figured it all out yet. But I'm getting close. And they know."

"Close to what?"

"That whore of yours. And who killed her."

Ned's entire body was vibrating. Sheer terror was coursing through him. I assumed this was his paranoia. This was the manifestation of his feelings toward his father. Wanda's death would have reactivated these emotions. Ned would then project them outwardly onto the nondescript "them."

"Who killed her?"

"I can't tell you," Ned said. "For your protection. But to stop me, they have to kill me."

Ned's jaw trembled. I could tell he could barely contain the thoughts racing through his head.

"Have you gone to the police?"

Ned removed his sunglasses and raised his eyebrows. "You expect me to trust Ernie Weagle? That sumbitch-"

"Ned, you're getting yourself worked up."

"Doc, this ain't paranoia. This is real. I'm close and I'll blow the lid off this."

He kept his voice quiet and spoke with a steady, almost measured cadence. Usually when Ned's paranoia was ramping up he became more disorganized, ranting and raving. This was different.

"What you did there, with those pigs, not tellin' them nothin' about what you know about that whore."

"Ned, please have some respect-"

"-that she's fucking Barrington. Also a patient of yours."

"Ned."

"That she's pimped by Getson. You could've told 'em. But you didn't. You told all of 'em to go fuck themselves. That you ain't saying shit. So yeah, I know you're one I can trust."

"Joe and Buddy and-"

"It's not them, Doc. She was fucking someone else."

"Tell me then, who?"

He shook his head. "I'm here 'cause if they get me, my investigation doesn't die. Don't trust those pigs to solve this. In the old school bus on my property there's a safe. I'm gonna tell you the combo."

"Can you write it down?"

"No." Ned looked at me sharply. "No paper trail. Don't you go writing it down."

"Ned, I think you're overreacting. A lot happened, you found her dead. That's shocking and-"

"Zero-six-"

"Ned."

"Zero-two."

"Come on."

"Repeat it, Doc, so I know you've got it."

I repeated the numbers.

"Wait, isn't that the year that Newton-"

"When the smartest man in history says world's ending on that date, I can't disagree."

I didn't have it in me to tell Ned that Newton didn't predict the world would end in 2060. Rather he said the world wouldn't end *before* 2060.

"I ain't afraid to go down. No one comes to my town and starts killing people. Even whores."

Ned put his sunglasses and hat back on. He flipped up his hood.

"Wish me luck. Don't forget those numbers."

Ned opened the door a crack, poked his head out, and looked up and down the hall before slipping out. I reached for the pad of paper to write the numbers down, but Sheila walked in.

"Ned's weirder than usual."

"He discovered Wanda," I said. "It's stressed him."

Sheila sat down across from me. "It's stressed you, sweetheart. You're not letting yourself grieve. I miss Wanda too."

I ignored Sheila's comment. "Wanda was going to meet Randy last night. Police say he has an alibi, but-" I ran my hand down my beard. "Confidential?"

Sheila nodded. She was part of my office staff, so she could be privy to some information discussed in session, on a need-to-know basis. And Sheila was a vault; she knew my patients, so she was a perfect sounding board.

"I mean, Randy had a motive. She put him away with her testimony. Who else would have as strong a reason to kill her?"

"Well, a lot of men. Wives too. And aren't the sheriffs tracing the casing?"

I swallowed. It bothered me that my gun was missing. I thought of what Doug said. Randy could have broken in when my cabin was empty after the fire and taken it. But Randy didn't have a car, so he would've had to come to my place with someone else or borrowed a vehicle.

"They can't trace it. Most guns aren't registered. Think about it, Sheila. He's killed before. He's an addict. He has a motive. The only thing that doesn't fit is that he has an alibi."

"The boy couldn't have done it, Gus."

"Why not?"

"Not that boy. Not his sister."

"What are you talking about?"

Sheila sighed, and spoke reluctantly. "I babysat the boy. Randy. And Wanda too. Before-"

"You knew Wanda?" Sheila the vault revealing yet another secret.

"That girl was a terror. Hormonal doesn't describe what that girl went through. Temper tantrums that'd make Jesus Christ himself wonder if Satan finally won."

That made me smile. Wanda had a fighting spirit. I saw it in her until the day she died.

"And those parents, boy oh boy. Not equipped to handle her. Mind you, they probably made her how she was."

Until the end, Wanda skirted around details of her relationship with her parents. She couldn't go there. Why would she? She'd already lived it once.

"But that boy was an angel."

I remembered Wanda talking about "little Randy." My mind grasped at a moment she described. A red tricycle. The image brought back the memory. Randy was on her old tricycle, tassels ripped off one of the handles. Wanda had taught him how to pedal. And Randy was racing out to the end of the driveway toward the highway just as a truck was approaching. Wanda noticed, sprinted over, and pushed him off the tricycle and into the drainage ditch. He knocked his head against the culvert, splitting it open. He probably needed stitches, but nobody bothered to take him to a doctor.

Her mom then proceeded to beat the shit out of her. First because she thought it was Wanda who hurt Randy. Then, once she found out that Wanda had saved Randy's life, she beat her again for not watching him closely enough.

And after, as Wanda was licking her wounds, little Randy came over, his head taped up. He brought her a Popsicle. Pink.

"He had these eyes that glowed. They were so alive. And he adored Wanda, Gus. She was the embodiment of life to him. She was momma to him. He even called her mommy."

I remembered Wanda telling me that as well. And the whipping her mother laid on her when she heard him say that.

"Those two were given no chance. Good-for-nothing mother." Sheila's nostrils flared. There was an anger in her that I hadn't sensed before. "But kill Wanda?" She shook her head. "I'd sooner believe you killed her than Randy."

I was fairly sure Sheila was joking, but her words hung in the air. Her eyes darted between me and her hands in her lap. I reminded myself that Sheila was the only person on earth I fully trusted.

Sheila was seeing the boy on the red tricycle. She hadn't seen him grow into the petty criminal who graduated to the drug dealer, and then the addict. She hadn't seen him develop into the hit man who killed fellow gang members. Sheila was kind. She saw the good in people.

But I had to see for myself.

"Can you take me to him?"

"Who? Randy?"

"Yes. I want to talk to him."

Sheila shook her head. "Leave it to the police, Gus."

"Sheila, they asked me to help profile the killer. They want me to do this. Consider it police business."

"Like I'm supposed to believe that."

"He'll remember you. Maybe he can help us figure out who killed Wanda."

I sat in the passenger seat of Sheila's Chevy Malibu as we drove through downtown during Bridgetown's rush hour. I hadn't been through downtown in weeks. Along the bank of the wide Habe River, a few of the long-abandoned buildings had signs advertising that they were being renovated. The old Moffatt's Pharmacy was ditching the neon orange "Drugs" sign and converting to a cafe and wine bar. The red brick Moses Tea Factory's transformation into a craft brewery was well underway. A row of silver fermentation tanks stood in the front window. I wondered what the rent was and if I should move my practice into one of these character buildings. The view would be great.

We passed the old bowling alley that was being torn down to make way for a supermarket. I saw my patient Wesley Tate just inside the fence, wearing his preferred flannel shirt and trucker hat, rummaging through scrap wood and metal. Wes spent his days walking miles up and down the county's dirt roads, looking for junk piles to search through while chain-smoking cigarillos. It was never clear to me what Wes was looking for. I was never able to understand what psychological function the garbage-picking served. But it kept him active and focused for sixteen hours a day.

As we crossed the bridge over the river, I thought of something that Wanda once said to me: "It must have been nice having a mom who loved you."

Her words stung a part of me so deep that I ended the session only a few minutes later. I felt lightheaded, almost dizzy, and I remember little of the rest of the day. Since that day, my memory seemed to come and go in flashes.

It took me to the pink-and-white, floral-patterned, hard-stuffed chaise in my mother's office. Every day after school, starting in grade two, I lay there staring up at the drop ceiling while my mother, Dr. Margaret Fischer, sat behind demanding I free associate. She said it was necessary that I clear out any psychological cobwebs before I entered puberty, because my hormones would amplify any hang-ups I still had.

I can tell you that there were one thousand three hundred and twenty-six pin holes on the panel directly above the chaise. There were at least one thousand one hundred and forty-two on the panel next to it. I was never able to complete my count before Margaret would snap at me to focus.

When I was sixteen my mother asked me if my feelings for Carmen Rafuse—my first major crush—were simply a manifestation of the unresolved sexual feelings toward her. My mother thought that I was trapped in my oedipal longings for her. At that point I flat-out refused to be analyzed by my own mother. She responded with her common refrain: it was my dad's fault for abandoning me.

If I was sad, she'd ask if I felt rage toward my dad.

If I was mad, she'd ask if I was angry at her for denying me milk in infancy. But even that was my father's fault for not being around.

She wouldn't tell me what happened to my dad, except that he'd left and "abandoned" me.

She didn't know that I'd made a picture of him in my mind, a fantasy I intentionally excluded from my forced therapy sessions. He was my secret. Tall, strong, a trimmed beard and strong jaw, wavy hair swept back. He wore a dark jean jacket, plaid shirt, big belt buckle, and faded Levi's. He rode a motorcycle without a helmet. I assumed he rode that motorcycle to get as far away from my crazy mother as possible.

I resented this fantasy father at first, but as I got older I understood him and why he would leave my mother. Eventually, I grew envious of him and his freedom.

Alistair had entered my life when I was about eight. Even at the time, he was the most prominent analyst at the institute. Mother said he came to be a father figure to me. Alistair was married but had no kids. He wasn't anything like my imaginary rock 'n' roll dad. He was stiff, wore tweed sport coats around the house on Saturday mornings, had a fading British accent, dissected Greek tragedies, and actually enjoyed classical music.

But he sat with me, and taught me things with a patience I have not come across since. I became fluent in Latin with his tutelage, and together we would analyze the works of Julius Caesar and Cicero. We then focused on learning German, working our way through Freud's and Adler's early works. I even learned to hammer out Paganini's Concerto No.1 on the violin thanks to his even-tempered guidance.

One memory stuck out like a cancerous tumor in my mind. My dad was gone at least eight years at this time. I was about ten, and I came directly home from school for my analysis session. It was a warm early summer day. I was hot and thirsty. I knew I was not allowed into the main house at that time, only into my mother's office, which had a separate entrance. I opened her office door but she wasn't there.

I assumed she must have been running late, so I decided to go to the kitchen and quietly pour myself a big glass of water from the faucet. I made sure to only turn the tap halfway so that it didn't make too much noise. My mother wouldn't tolerate it. I gulped it down.

Down the hallway, there was a repetitive thumping followed by a snap. I could faintly hear a man yelping, followed by my mother's voice. She sounded like she was in distress.

I slipped off my shoes to reduce the chance of making noise and tiptoed down the hallway toward the sounds. I put my ear to my mother's bedroom door. The sounds continued. Thumping. Slapping. Yelping.

I turned the knob and let the door fall open a crack. My mother had her back to me. Dressed in leather undergarments and holding a whip, she was straddling Alistair, who was chained to the bed. She raised the whip and smacked it across his chest.

I turned to run, but in my panic my knee bumped into the door, opening it all the way and slamming it against the wall.

Alistair sat up. When he saw me, utter shame descended over his face.

My mother, on the other hand, calmly lifted herself off him and walked over to me, fully exposed. She calmly said, "You're not to come into the house after school. Now leave."

Then she turned and walked back to the bed. I let myself out.

Alistair never came back to the house. Years later, when I began training at the institute, he never addressed it. He must have hoped it was a childhood memory that faded away. I sure wish it had. My mother spoke about it once, saying, "Because you cannot follow directions, Alistair will not be coming back again."

We pulled up to Valhalla Suites, one of the only apartment blocks in Bridgetown. It was a six-unit, two-story, faded brick cube of a building. Two of the street numbers over the entrance had fallen off, but the outline was still visible. A garbage can stood out front, the ashtray on top full of cigarette butts.

I followed Sheila into the building. The smudged glass door slammed behind us. To our left, six tenants were listed on hand-written pieces of paper under the plastic sheet on the directory. Sheila ran her hand down the list until she found R. Flynn living in Unit 2. I pressed the button and listened to the ringing.

"Hello?" a voice crackled over the speaker. I motioned for Sheila to take the lead.

"It's Sheila. Sheila-"

"Sheila? Gustafson?"

"Yes. I'm here with Gus Young. We wanted to talk to you. About your sister."

Buzz. We entered the hallway. Despite the dim lighting, brown water stains were still visible on the walls and ceiling. It smelled like wet dog and dirty diapers. We passed the door for unit one, behind which a dog growled and scratched. We made our way to the far unit, and before we could knock, I heard the latch slide off.

The door opened. A man of about forty, with a wide, pock-marked face and long hair tucked behind his ears opened the door and smiled at us. He wore aviator-style glasses with thick lenses. A cross hung from his thin neck.

At the sight of Sheila he raised his hands, palms up, and looked to the heavens. He whispered a prayer of some sort and then threw his arms around her.

Randy pressed his face against Sheila's shoulder and wailed. Sheila put a hand on his back and glanced over at me, bemused, as though Randy's tears certified him innocent of Wanda's murder.

Randy pulled back, wiped his cheeks, and cleared his nose.

"The Lord works in mysterious ways." He pointed to the sky. "But he's got a plan for us. He's brought you to me."

"Randy, this is Gus Young, he's-"

Randy put a firm hand on the back of my neck and pulled me toward him until our foreheads touched.

"You were The Light, Doctor. You brought Light to her. I saw it in her like never before. You are an angel."

I took a step back and straightened to release myself from Randy's hold.

"I'm sorry for your loss, Randy."

"He wanted her back." Randy bit his lip and nodded slowly. "Come in."

The place was a bachelor unit, and only had two windows the size of a cereal box. The linoleum floors were curling at the seams and several of the kitchen cabinets were missing doors. There were almost no decorations except for a religious calendar hanging on the wall next to a simple cross.

He led us to a wood veneer dining table with two chairs. An armchair rested against the window beside a coffee table with the King James Bible. Randy dragged the armchair over, insisting that Sheila take it. The place was devoid of any other furniture.

Randy offered us water because he had nothing else. I said yes, because these reborn Christian criminals made me nauseous and I thought a drink would help calm my stomach. I'd seen this type of persona over and over again when I worked forensic cases. Jesus forgave, so these criminals figured all they had to do was take him in and all of their badness would be erased. They never bothered to accept that a monster lurked inside them. This was a form of primitive denial that I found almost impossible to break through. But if the reality that evil lived in them ever entered their conscious awareness, their whole facade would crumble. That internal beast would become stronger than ever and maybe even swallow them up.

The water came to me in a dirty glass but I still sipped it to be polite. I needed information and I didn't want to insult him.

"Sheila, you have no idea what it means for me to see your spirit on a day like today."

"I remember, dear, how much Wanda meant to you. Since you were like this." She held her hand three feet off the ground.

Randy broke down, taking off his glasses and placing them on the table.

"All those years, while I was doing my time, I worried that Wanda was torturing herself for my incarceration. She did the right thing. So I prayed every day that He would give me the gift of seeing my sister once again. And He did."

"You saw Wanda yesterday?" I said.

"And she was beautiful. Even more than before. And I think you did that, Dr. Young. You let her feel safe enough to let the Light out."

"Thanks," I said abruptly. I wanted to get Randy on track. "So you met her yesterday?"

"Yes."

"When, approximately?"

"Six o'clock. I went to her house."

"How long were you there?"

Randy smiled, looked at Sheila and then me. "Doctor, I've already talked to the police. I understand that I'd be a suspect. But with the Lord as my witness, I would never, ever, hurt my sister. Or anyone for that matter."

"Well, you've killed, Randy. Let's not forget that."

Randy's jaw went a bit slack. I'd knocked him down a couple of spiritual pegs.

"And your sister was afraid of visiting you."

"I know. She didn't know what to expect. What my reaction would be. But we got through that quickly."

"You forgave her."

He curled his lips as though I'd said something offensive. "There was nothing to forgive. Wanda did the right thing. I killed Jimmy Getson. I took a man's life. I needed to repent."

As teenagers, Randy was best friends with Buddy Getson. At that time, Buddy's father Jimmy ran the crime ring. When Randy and Jimmy butted heads, Randy ended up killing him and dumping the body in Ernie Weagle's junkyard. Rumor had it that their argument started because Jimmy wanted Randy to kill Ernie, who had since become the town sheriff.

Wanda testifying against Randy actually saved two lives. If she didn't testify against her brother, Buddy would have had her killed. And she saved Randy's life, because if he wasn't in custody, Buddy would have killed him too.

"What about Buddy Getson? Did you talk to him?"

"No." Randy paused and tightened his lips before taking a sip of water. "I don't know if I have the strength. Yet."

"The strength to stare down your old friend whose dad you murdered?"

"You're not afraid to go to certain places, are you?"

"It's kind of my job, Randy. To go to any emotional place."

"There's a dark hole there. One the angels themselves try to forget about."

"Randy, I go where angels fear to tread."

Randy forced a shallow laugh, avoiding eye contact as he stood up. He put his glass down beside the sink.

"Wanda told me that Buddy wasn't going to come after me. That he understood what I'd done. That he was happy his daddy was gone." He refilled his glass under the tap. "Now that's sad."

"What did you talk about with Wanda?" Sheila interjected, as though I'd fallen too far off the mark with my interrogation of Randy.

"We talked for hours. We sat by the bonfire in front of her place until it was dark. She mostly asked about me. How I'd kicked the pills. What jail was like, what I was going to do now that I was out. Big sister stuff. She was looking out for me like she always did."

"Did she mention anything that makes you wonder who might have done this to her?" Sheila said.

He shook his head. "Like I told the sheriff and the lady cop-" He snapped his fingers.

"Debbie."

"Debbie, right. Wanda told me she was soon getting out of the escort business and settling down. She seemed happy." Randy paused. "You know, Wanda did say this guy—she called him a 'long-haired freak'—had been driving by, spying on her."

"She was worried about this person?" I said.

"I wouldn't say, not really. I was just telling her about some of the people I'd met in prison, crazy guys. She mentioned it to me in passing."

"Did she say who it was?" I immediately thought of Night Hawk Ned.

"Nope." Randy's shoulders drooped, like he was weighed down. "Getting out, I thought I'd set this all right, fix my relationships. I never thought He would test me like this. But whoever did this, I'll find it." He pointed at his heart. "I'll find it in my heart to forgive."

I opened the door to Sheila's car, swept away the crumbs and colored sprinkles that had fallen off the donut I'd eaten on the way out. Sheila sat down and adjusted her rear-view mirror, then started up the Malibu and pulled out onto the road.

"Who do you think he was talking about?" I said.

"I thought of Ned."

"Driving around. Spying. Crazy hair."

"You don't think?"

"No," I said. And I meant it. Ned was an odd person, but he saw himself firmly as a protector, a purveyor of justice. If anything, Ned would have wanted to protect her, and he was watching her because he thought she was in danger.

As we drove, a flash of memory came back to me. Maybe a year ago, Ned said that he was worried about "that whore." He'd shut me down before I could probe further.

But maybe Ned knew something more. Maybe Ned had a lead on who could have killed Wanda. Maybe he was being followed.

Ned was such a wildcard that I felt silly hanging my hat on one of his conspiracy theories. But my gun was missing and the sheriff had found a matching casing at the murder scene. If I didn't find out who killed Wanda, I could soon be in the frame.

Before talking to Ned, I decided I needed background information.

"I need to get back to the office to check my notes." I looked at my watch. The store was already closed. "Can you let me in?"

14

As the head of customer service at Buck's, Sheila had the master keys. So even though it was after hours, she was able to unlock the front door and turn off the alarms. The store was dark, but a few security lights gave off enough glow that I was able to make my way to the back hallway. Sheila said she would wait at the customer service desk.

On the way to my office, I realized I was starving. I put a quarter in the dusty vending machine beside the washrooms and twisted the dial until a fistful of M&M's spilled out.

I opened my office door, turned on the Tiffany lamp beside my chair, and pulled Ned's blue shadow files from the safe.

I was as satisfied as I could be that Randy hadn't killed Wanda. His emotions seemed genuine enough, and that, combined with his alibi, made me agree with the sheriff's department that he was no longer a credible suspect. If the person stalking Wanda was Ned, it gave me an important lead. However, I wanted to corroborate the story before approaching him.

I had often wondered whether keeping shadow notes on my

patients was a waste of time, but as the years passed and my memory became more spotty, they came in handy. I flipped through the pages, quickly scanning entries for any key words. The problem was that Ned's thought processes were paranoid and his suspiciousness drifted from person to person, so the entries were equally disorganized. The notes looked like a dog's breakfast of conspiracy theories.

Then I came across it. An entry from six months earlier.

Worried that a fellow patient (female) is in danger.

Strong Urge/impulse to protect. Watches from a distance. Preoccupied.

? Represents projection of internalized anger outwardly onto an unknown male object?

? Projects internalized fearful/helpless child onto her?

Entertains alternative explanations. Seems to fit in his paranoid character structure.

I wished the notes were more detailed, but they pointed to Ned's concern about another patient, enough that he could have been compelled to stake out Wanda's home. Enough that she was freaked out enough to tell Randy.

I'd interpreted his concern about Wanda's safety as a mere projection. I didn't take his description as a credible threat to her. In Ned's internal world, someone was always in danger. If he wasn't worried about Wanda, it could have been Sheila, the gas station attendant, anyone. But even a broken clock was right twice a day.

I locked his file in the wall vault and walked to customer service, where Sheila was flipping through a grocery store flyer.

"I'm all done. I'm going to see Ned."

"Do you need me to come along?"

"No, I'll do this myself. It would frighten him if you came."

"What about letting Ernie handle this, Gus? You're just taking this too hard. You're getting all wrapped up."

"Sheila." I put my hand on top of hers. "I'm fine. But I can help figure this out. Because I know both Ned and Wanda, I might be able to get some information that the police can't."

Part of me wanted to tell Sheila about the other half of my motivation to find out who killed Wanda. I trusted that Sheila would keep any information I gave her about my missing gun a secret, but that would put her in the unfair position of having to withhold information from police.

"Plus," I said, "Ned is off-the-charts paranoid right now. Consider it part wellness check. Okay?"

"You're the boss."

"Sheila, we both know you run the show."

———

Sheila dropped me off at the Oarhouse, where I got in my truck and drove to Ned's alone. The moonless sky was turning crimson above the trees, then bled to magenta and dark purple. The empty highway was a black ribbon winding through the forest. I flicked on my brights, but even that gave me only fifteen yards of road. I saw vehicle headlights behind me, but they disappeared, likely turning off to a home in the woods.

Even though I was fifteen minutes out of downtown, this was still considered part of Bridgetown. In fact, more towns-people lived off little highways like this than in the town proper. The difference was that the further you got toward the edge of the town limits, the more trust for police and government dropped, and the more gun ownership and ATV injuries increased. And Ned lived just past the town limit.

I nearly missed Ned's driveway. I had to press hard on the brakes to avoid ending up in the ditch. The marker for his home was nothing more than a stick bearing the numbers 39. His dirt driveway seemed to stop at the wood's edge. A set of deer antlers tied around a birch tree confirmed this was Ned's place.

I pulled onto the driveway and was immediately met with three bright-red *No Trespassing* signs. Ned had mentioned setting booby traps around his property, but I decided that I would take my chances. My truck tilted and bounced over every pothole as I made my way deeper along the narrow drive barely wide enough for me to pass. Branches screeched as they scraped along the sides of my truck.

Eventually the driveway widened, and to the right was a long pile of stacked firewood. Above, a plywood sign was hammered into a tree with the spray-painted words *Steal Wood = Jail*.

Off in the distance, I made out a rusty old school bus. Inside must be the safe Ned told me about that contained clues of his investigation.

Ahead was a western-style cabin with a corrugated metal roof overhanging a porch. The cedar siding was weathered gray. Solar panels stood on the roof and a windmill spun at the peak. I remembered when Ned got the panels. He didn't buy them because he was an environmentalist—he thought climate change was a hoax perpetrated by the oil companies. Rather he had solar panels to remain off grid and keep the government out of his affairs. When the contractor wanted to connect the panels to the town grid, as was standard practice, Ned chased him off his property and demanded that he sell him the panels in cash. Ned then installed them himself.

A light was on inside. As soon as I turned off the truck and the headlights dimmed, the inside light flicked off too. I walked up to the front porch and looked up. One surveillance camera pointed at the front door, another toward the yard. I wondered if Ned generated enough power to run them. But knowing Ned, any available kilowatts would first be directed to the cameras.

No smoke was coming from the chimney, despite the forty-degree temperature. Ned must have been freezing inside. But I sense that he was too paranoid that someone might notice smoke and realize he was home.

I gave a few good raps on the screen door and waited. No answer. The curtains on the front window fluttered. I saw a faint glare through the window. As I moved closer, I realized that Ned was staring out the window, motionless, his face wrapped in the curtain. The glare was coming off his sunglasses. I was surprised that he hadn't hidden in one of the foxholes he had dug under the living room floor.

I moved over to the window, pressing my face against the glass.

"Ned, it's me. Gus Young," I yelled.

I could hear him stumble. A pot crashed to the floor. Then the front door flew open.

"Quiet down, Doc."

"Ned, I'm-"

"Shh." He had one finger to his mouth and waved me inside with his other hand. He looked both ways before he closed the door and flipped three deadbolts. Then he ripped off his sunglasses.

"Can't be comin' in like this, buddy. Things are getting heated and out of control. They know I'm getting close and they're getting nervous, nervous, running their guns, watching us, not just me but now they got you in the crosshairs too, Doc. It's us against them now."

"Ned, who are we against?"

"Not yet, not yet." Ned was bouncing on his toes. "They've stepped into the net, one foot in, hoppin', hoppin', then when they get the other in..." He smashed his fist on the table. "We tighten the noose. They got the whore but they don't get us."

"Ned you've got to calm down."

"Oh, I'm calm, buddy, calm, calm." He held his hand out to show me it was steady, but his fingers fluttered like the last fall leaf clinging to a twig. Ned wouldn't be aware that he was nervous. His mind operated on denial. Every emotion he experienced he perceived as coming from outside of himself. He wasn't scared, he would say; the world was dangerous.

"You're calm as a cucumber."

"Ready for anything." He smiled with wild eyes.

I looked around Ned's place. Stacks of newspapers that reached the light switches lined the walls, narrowing the hallways so you'd have to walk through sideways. Newspaper clippings were taped to the walls haphazardly. Permanent red marker was scrawled across them, creating a maze of circles and connecting arrows. Dirty pots and plates filled the kitchen sink.

Beside the living room couch stood a full-size taxidermy buck. Along plate rails were rows of antlers that Night Hawk had picked up along the highway. He always kept the antlers as a memorial to the dead animals.

"Ned, I need to ask you something." I motioned to the kitchen table, full of newspapers, magazines, and a half-whittled stick. "Can I sit down?"

He shook his head. "No, Doc. I like you, but this is my place and you're only inside for your protection, 'cause it ain't safe out there for-"

"Ned, I need to know if yesterday morning was the first time you were at Wanda's place?"

"You saying I was in there doing that whore? No, no, you have me wrong, I'm not that, I treat women with respect, the fairer sex, they need our protection." He slapped my chest and then his own like we were bros. "I don't pay to get my dick-"

"Ned, stop." His sense of chivalry was as progressive as a

Viking conqueror's. "I'm not saying you were a client. Just if you were ever there. Nearby."

Ned squinted at me and tilted his head. "What are you saying?"

"A year ago you mentioned watching one of my patients from a distance. That you felt she was in danger."

He was still squinting without blinking, as though he didn't remember the conversation.

"And I met with her brother Randy. He said that she was worried someone was spying on her. And the description, well, was similar to-"

Ned pointed a finger right in my face. His neck veins popped up. "You treasonous son of a bitch!"

"Ned, I-"

"What we talk about is confidential. You promised me! And now you go and talk to that whore's murderous brother about me? I'll have your license revoked. I knew I couldn't trust you. 'Ned, but he's a good guy, he's honest.' Bullshit. Lying right to my face." He was hyperventilating. "Accusing me? You think I killed her?"

"No, Ned, I-"

"Night Hawk don't have no guns. Night Hawk's a pacifist. He keeps the peace. Go find a gun in here. Look around."

Ned had the strictest moral code I had ever encountered. It was completely rigid and unique. He didn't pay taxes because he didn't think the government had moral authority over him. But murder was simply not in his psyche. No. Ned's manner of operating was out of fear; he would run and hide before lashing out. He was too terrified to be able to hurt anyone.

"Ned, I'm sorry. I don't think you killed Wanda." I put a finger in his face now. "And I didn't tell anyone anything about you. That's my code."

He scanned me up and down and then nodded with approval.

"We find the murder weapon for the .303, then I get this solved before Weagle can, before that corrupt bastard even gets the autopsy results back."

I thought of the gun, and who could have taken it from my home. Was it too late to report it missing?

"Ned, who do you think could have done this?"

"No. Not yet. I can't tell you yet. But you've gotta go, before they see you with me. For your protection."

"Ned."

"If I tell you, I put you in danger."

Ned was putting his foot down and there was no way he would share anything else. But he seemed to feel certain that he was close to finding Wanda's killer, so I decided to find out what I could.

"Can I use your washroom before I go?"

"You can piss outside."

"Really?"

He exhaled. "Down the hall and out the door is the outhouse. No bathroom inside. Don't have enough water for that kind of luxury."

I walked to the hall, turned sideways, and shuffled between the rows of yellowed newspapers. Just before I reached the screen door leading outside, a closed door with a line of light at the bottom caught my eye. It was curious, because Ned was keeping the rest of his house dark yet somehow overlooked this room.

I looked behind me. Ned was out of my sight line in the kitchen, so I pushed the door open. The room was narrow with a low-wattage bulb overhead. A long desk ran along the wall, and a fly-tying apparatus was clamped to the edge. Next to it was a pile of Polaroid photos. I stepped inside and picked them up.

They were slightly faded pictures of a house taken from a road. The house had teal shutters and a beautiful garden. A white Cavalier was parked out front in one of them. I rifled through the rest. These were pictures of Wanda's trailer.

I quickly stepped out of the room, pushed the screen door, and let it slam closed so Ned would think that I had gone to the outhouse. Then I slipped back into the room.

Ned was lying to me. He had been watching Wanda's house. If he'd lied about stalking Wanda, could he be lying about killing her? Still, the pictures showed that he was surveying her, maybe as part of his need to protect her. Her death would leave him with guilt. But because of his personality structure, he would channel any guilty feelings into a crusade to solve the murder.

No, Ned couldn't have.

I turned to leave. What I saw hanging from the inside door knob made me feel like the floor was going to cave in.

A turquoise stone.

At the center of a silver cross.

Wanda's necklace.

I lifted it off the knob and held it.

He'd killed her. I'd mistaken the cause of his paranoia as the stress of finding Wanda dead. Instead, this paranoia was a manifestation of guilt over killing her. Now he was projecting that guilt outwardly, and completely denying reality. He wasn't paranoid. He was a murderer.

The necklace shook in my hand. I felt heat pulsate under my skin.

I floated out of the room, gliding between the stacks of newspapers until I reached Ned. I squeezed the cross between my fingers until the edges drew blood, then held it in front of Ned's face.

"You fucking killer."

Ned stiffened. His eyes bulged.

"You killed her. You crazy animal."

"No, no-"

"You lied to me." I spoke through my teeth. "You killed and then you lied. You killer."

Any remaining bravado drained from Ned's face. Fear overcame him, and I saw the eyes of a little boy who'd found his dad dead.

"I didn't, I, I, I didn't, please. Believe me!" He covered his ears, closed his eyes, and fell to his knees.

"And you took this as a souvenir." I squeezed Wanda's necklace in my fist and punched Ned twice in the face, knocking him onto the floor.

"No, I didn't, please." He looked up at me, pleading.

"Where'd you get the gun, Ned? How'd you get it?"

"No, I didn't."

"You break in? When? Where?"

He shook his head.

"I wanted to protect her," he whimpered. "I was coming back to check on her. She was so, so vulnerable. And I found her on the road." He broke down into stuttering sobs.

"You did it."

"No, no, I didn't. Please believe me, Doc."

"Then why? Why the necklace?"

"So I don't forget." His eyes were angry now.

"Forget what?"

"That I failed! I failed her. I couldn't save her."

I took a deep breath and watched Ned. His entire external persona seemed to have dissolved into a puddle, a man destroyed, left in ruins on the floor. I'd smashed his veneer of denial, the only psychological protective mechanism he had. I'd killed the spirit that lived in him.

Nausea spread through me and I left, stumbling out of the house, tripping off the stairs onto his driveway. I found my way to the truck, then tossed the necklace onto the passenger seat, threw it in reverse, and peeled away.

15

I recalled coming home, throwing up twice, and stumbling into bed. For the first time in months I slept hard and didn't remember the night. I woke up at 8:57 a.m. to Anna whimpering beside the door to go out. Although I had a long sleep, my head still felt woolly, and I felt like I could stay in bed for another eight hours. I had forgotten to take my nighttime pills, so my back was pinching and the back of my leg burned.

I rolled out of bed, threw on my housecoat and slippers, and opened the sliding door. I wandered over to the kitchen, filled the kettle, and waited for the water to boil on the gas stove. When the kettle whistled I poured the water into a mug, added two tablespoons of instant coffee, and made my way to the deck.

It was autumn-crisp and steam rose up from the still lake like a thick fog. Anna stood by the shore, lapping up water. A skein of geese flew across the overcast sky, headed south, running from the cold as fast as they could. I sat on a patio chair and put my feet up on the railing.

Ned. All those years I'd never really taken him seriously, viewing him as a caricature to be tamed rather than a whole person to be respected. I'd failed him. The thought made my throat tighten.

How hard had I hit him? Did it matter? I tried to rationalize like an abusive husband: my fist wasn't completely closed, so it wasn't that bad.

It was as though with that punch, I sent my fist cracking right through Ned's psyche, leaving nothing but a helpless little boy alone on the floor. I'd destroyed who he was. It must have been incomprehensible to him to have the one person he trusted be the very person who hurt him.

I didn't want that tantrum-that violence-to be me. But that rage lived in me. Wanda's death activated the part of me I'd forgotten existed. An almost irrational need to protect her. So powerful that I'd trampled and spat all over my duty to help Ned. Why did Wanda mean so much to me?

I didn't, as a rule, do nasty things. Even Meg would agree with that. Through the whole divorce, I never resorted to the tit-for-tat nastiness that seemed to characterize most modern separations. I kept it transactional. She wanted the house? She got the house. I wanted my books. She got the car. Karen blamed me for the breakdown of the marriage. But even with my daughter I never strayed from a level-headed, rational approach.

I must also have a dark side if I am to be whole, Jung said. It was as though I'd ignored that part of me. But intimately understanding that darkness was the very thing that would allow me to deal with the darkness of others. I was merely afraid to look in the mirror, and Ned became the casualty.

I took a sip of coffee and it tasted acidic, burning as it went down.

Ned wasn't easy to deal with. But in his own way, he only wanted good to happen. I wasn't sure I could confidently say the same for myself.

The man I saw curled up on the floor didn't murder Wanda.

Of this I was certain. He was naked and vulnerable; there was nothing left of him. There was no rage, just terror and loss. He felt he'd failed Wanda. Just as I did.

If not Ned, then who? Joe denied involvement. I had no idea if the sheriff's department was even looking at him. Ned had mentioned that Buddy was coming around Wanda's house. Did he have a vendetta against Randy and murder her as retribution?

My cell phone buzzed twice, so I went inside and picked it up.

"Gus Young?"

"Yes."

"This is John Knox from the fire department. Just wanted to let you know that we got the report back and your home is clear to return to, as long as you stay out of the boarded-up area. Electricity is back on."

I flicked on the kitchen light to test it. "Thank you."

I didn't bother telling him that I had already spent two nights in my bed in case that was some kind of code violation.

"We were able to salvage some of your old records and the player. I left them in a box out front."

I hung up and walked around to the front of my house, then ripped open the cardboard box sitting there. A half dozen vinyl records were still inside, which made me smile a bit.

My phone buzzed and I saw that I had several missed text messages from last night, all from Renee.

Are you close?

Forget about me?

I'm getting worried.

And last,

I'm going to bed. It's been a long time since I've been stood up.

I had completely forgotten about my plans with Renee. After she drove my inebriated self home, I wanted to make things up to her, so my timing couldn't have been worse. I decided it was best to call her immediately and apologize rather than delay.

"Hello?"

"Am I too late to apologize?"

A pause. "Depends on where you were. Or who you were with."

"It was completely accidental." I sighed. "I was dealing with a crisis. With a patient, and I just forgot." It was sort of true, I figured. I left out that the crisis was of my own making.

"What happened?"

"I can't tell you. It's confidential."

"Convenient."

"Trust me. I would have much rather been with you last night than where I was."

"I believe you."

"You do?"

"Well, why would you stand me up, right? I'm fun, funny, charming, beautiful-"

There was a sharpness in her voice that made me briefly question whether she was joking, but I thought it was best to play along. "And that's being modest," I said.

"Well, Doctor, you have certainly beaten me in the charm department."

Renee had an ability to make me smile. I'd briefly forgotten all about my altercation with Ned.

"So, what are you going to do to make it up to me?"

I puffed out my cheeks and let out a breath as I looked at my kitchen. The addition was still boarded up, but now that the electricity was connected, it was fully functional.

"I'll make you dinner. My place."

"Your place? Is it safe?"

"Volunteer firefighters say so."

She paused. "Well, inviting me to your place a second time is a bit forward, but I like a man who's bold. And you have a nice behind. What's on the menu?"

"I recently caught some venison."

"Well, you appear to have figured out that the way to a woman's heart is with... wild game."

"If you like it, I'll consider us soul mates."

She chuckled.

"I'll see you tonight."

Anna had run around the cabin and was barking at the end of the driveway. I wondered if Herman was wandering over.

I was about to put my phone down when I noticed that I had a voicemail. I played it as I walked to the driveway.

"Hi... Dad. Just confirming about tomorrow. I have a car, so I can just come by your place around seven. Maybe just keep your phone on in case I need directions."

I pressed my fist against my forehead. I had forgotten Karen was coming over for dinner, which meant I had to cancel again with Renee. I wondered how long she would put up with me before she told me to take a hike.

Anna suddenly sprinted past me up the driveway to stand beside the road and bark incessantly.

I followed her, and when I reached the driveway I looked up the road. Two sheriff's cruisers were barreling toward me, kicking up dust clouds behind them. They didn't have lights or sirens on, which made me wonder why they were driving so quickly. They stopped on the shoulder, blocking my driveway. I put my coffee mug on the driveway, got Anna on a leash, and commanded her to quiet down.

Debbie Parks got out of one cruiser and Ernie Weagle the other.

Anna strained on the leash so I held her by the collar, but she kept jumping and barking wildly.

"Morning, Ernie. Debbie."

They exchanged glances. Debbie stopped five yards in front of me and promptly looked at her feet, deferring to Ernie, who came closer.

"Doc, uh, Gus." He crossed his arms and avoided eye contact. "We need you to come in."

"Okay, sure," I said. "Let me get changed and then I can meet you there?"

"I'm afraid you need to come with us."

"You're arresting me?"

"No." Ernie shuffled his feet. "You're a person of interest and we need a statement."

"Guys, Wanda is-"

"It's not Wanda." He looked up. "Ned Gamble was found dead in his home late last night."

16

The Bridgetown sheriff's detachment was a single-story brick building the size of a small grade school, too large for the size of town it operated in. It sat on an expanse of grass, alone on the edge of the town. A single cruiser was parked in front when we arrived. I followed Ernie and Debbie into the building.

Ernie had me sit in the reception area. It consisted of eight seats welded together beside a table littered with pamphlets for reporting poaching, illegal burning, and drunk driving.

The receptionist had her hair up in a bun with a pencil stuck through it. She didn't look at me, just sat at her desk furiously typing behind bulletproof glass. I wondered why they required the glass. In Bridgetown, everyone knew where everyone else lived. If someone wanted someone else dead, they could do it elsewhere and have a better chance of getting away with it.

Ernie said he needed to get some paperwork together before taking my statement. I'd asked him half a dozen times on the ride over if I was under arrest. Despite his assurances that I wasn't, the formality with which he had picked me up-two cruisers, two officers, official statements, a formal interview-made me realize that I was their suspect.

He wouldn't tell me anything about how Ned died. "Active investigation," he said. I knew that if they reviewed Ned's security cameras, they could place me at the scene. But they were clear that they weren't arresting me, which meant there was something more to the story.

I could have killed Ned last night. Seeing Wanda's necklace caused a moment of rage that overcame me with such force that I had no idea how I stopped myself after only two punches. It was the feeling of betrayal, the idea that Ned had somehow duped me, that made me furious.

But Ned was dead. I thought of him lying on the floor pleading with me. His last moments were sheer agony, a man broken. If he'd lived, I'm not sure how he could have psychologically recovered from the damage I caused.

It was a dereliction of my duty to help him.

There seemed to be two possibilities. The first was that Ned had shot Wanda and someone else had killed him, perhaps as retribution for Wanda's death. I immediately thought of Randy.

But after my confrontation with Ned, I couldn't reasonably believe he killed Wanda. Which meant someone else had. And that someone might have taken my gun. Could the same person have killed Ned? He'd said that he was close to figuring out Wanda's killer, and mentioned both Buddy and Joe.

Debbie Parks walked up to the door beside the receptionist and buzzed it open.

"Doctor Young, you can come in now."

I followed Debbie past the cubicles and down a hall into a room marked *Interview 1*. She held the door for me and I sat down at a small, scratched table holding a laptop and microphone. The walls were stark white but had black scuff marks around the bottom. A window looked out into a hallway. Debbie sat across from me and placed a legal pad and pen in front of her.

Her hair was pulled back tightly into a low bun. She wore minimal makeup aside from a swipe of mascara and was devoid of any jewelry. She had the rigid posture and demeanor of an ex-service person. She was simultaneously warm and distant, as though she were looking at me from a hundred yards away.

After getting my consent, she pressed the button on the tape recorder and asked me to state my tombstone data.

"Dr. Young, can you tell me where you were yesterday, October 16, between five p.m. and midnight?"

"I believe I was in my office in Buck's Hardware."

"The building closes at five, does it not?"

"Yes, it does. But an employee let me in."

"Sheila Gustafson?"

"Yes. Sheila was with me."

"Is it usual for you to be in your office after hours?"

"Not typically."

"Why did you go yesterday?"

"To check a file."

I remembered going into the office to check Ned's file. I realized that the rest of the night was fuzzy.

"Whose file?"

"A patient's. It's confidential."

"And you stayed there for the night?"

"No. I didn't stay long."

"Where did you go?"

"I went to Ned Gamble's place."

"He was a patient of yours?"

I hesitated. Although Ned was dead, he was still my patient. As far as I was concerned, Debbie didn't need to know that.

"I'm not able to tell you who my patients are. Confidential."

"Okay. Can you tell me why you went there?"

That information would essentially confirm Ned as one of my patients. I had to proceed cautiously. "I went to ask him something."

"Care to elaborate?"

"No."

"Even if—hypothetically speaking, Doctor—Mr. Gamble was a patient of yours, telling me about this as part of a murder investigation is not just permitted, it's required."

"That's not correct."

Debbie stopped writing and looked up at me.

"It's a common misunderstanding among law enforcement that as soon as a crime is committed the therapist-patient confidentiality is effectively void," I explained. "But the truth is that confidentiality remains intact unless it is, according to case law, 'more probable than not that a person is at risk of imminent harm to self or others.'"

It was also a common misconception among therapists. Typically, the moment a police officer or lawyer asked for records as part of a criminal investigation, therapists got nervous and handed over everything—an ethical violation on the therapists' part and damaging to the patient.

But no court would ever fault the therapist. The courts still had the archaic notion that being mentally ill generally meant the person was incapable of providing valid consent.

"I could get a warrant."

"And I'd have to read it."

I had no trouble staring down law enforcement officers. While spending years shuttling from courtroom to courtroom to testify as an expert witness, I'd endured tedious cross-examinations with bullheaded lawyers who tried to turn my nuanced opinions into something black-and-white. A district attorney once said to me, "So you're telling me, Dr. Young, that there is no objective way to quantify a person's risk to re-offend? That it's just a guess. That your profession is 'a series of educated guesses.' Is that what you're telling me?" I cleared my throat and said into the microphone, "That's precisely what I'm telling you." She looked at me as though I had offended her firstborn.

I saw the same look on Debbie's face. Law enforcement worked in absolutes, in binaries. A crime was either committed or it wasn't. People were guilty or they weren't.

But humans inhabited a world of infinite possibilities. They had endless motives and drives for their behavior. There was no limit to the lies they told others or themselves. In my world there were no absolutes. And so if I'm asked to keep a secret, I keep the damn secret.

Debbie inhaled so deeply through her nose that it whistled.

"Ned was shot dead last night, in his house. We came to the scene three hours after the estimated time of death." She punched a few keys on the laptop and spun it around so that we could both see it. A frozen video frame was on the screen, footage from one of the cameras on Ned's porch looking down at his front stairs. I could see my truck parked ten yards ahead at the edge of the screen.

"Mr. Gamble kept surveillance footage running twenty-four hours a day. We were able to pull this from his camera last night."

She pushed play, and I could see myself scrambling off Ned's porch and tripping onto the driveway before getting into my truck and racing away. If there was ever a guilty-looking exit, this was it.

"This was at 10:36 p.m." She pressed pause. "Could you explain this?"

I realized I had to offer something. "We had an altercation." I sighed. "We had a disagreement, things escalated, and I struck him."

"Struck him?"

"I punched him. Twice. In the head."

"What happened then?"

"He fell to the ground. I felt terrible about what I did and I left."

"Was he injured?"

"He was holding his jaw, yes. But if you're asking if he was still alive, yes, he was."

Debbie wrote down a few notes. "What was your disagreement about?"

"I can't say."

"Can't or won't?"

"It won't be said. For reasons that I can't tell you."

"You know, Dr. Young, you're the last known person to see Mr. Gamble alive. And we all know he was a patient of yours. We found appointment cards in his home. So, by trying to adhere to this pledge of secrecy, you could be incriminating yourself."

"Understood." I nodded.

Debbie rubbed her temple subtly, a sign of annoyance with me. "Where did you go afterward? Can you tell me that much?"

"I went home."

"Straight home?"

I paused. I remembered little of that night after leaving Ned's house. I had trouble remembering getting home. It's as though the time from leaving Ned's house to waking in the morning was plucked from my memory.

"Straight," I doubled down.

"No stopping? For gas, a friend's place?"

"Nope. Not to my recollection."

"Does your memory ever fail you, Doctor? Debbie was

staring directly at me. I thought of how she found me lost on the logging road.

"No, I'm good." There was a long pause. I sensed a pending "gotcha" moment, but it didn't come.

Something struck me then. Why wasn't I under arrest? I had an altercation with Ned, I was being evasive, I was the last person at his house.

"Did you go back to Mr. Gamble's house after that?"

"No, why?"

"Part of our investigation is also confidential."

I realized that something else must have happened after I left.

"Any other questions?"

"No, Doctor. But I need you to stay in the county, in case we have to ask you more questions as the investigation evolves."

"I didn't kill Ned. I think you know that, but I want it on the record."

"It's on the record." She tapped the microphone, then looked at me again. "Actually, just a few last questions. Do you own a rifle that shoots 0.303 cartridges?"

I felt blood drain from my face. Ned was found shot and now she was asking about cartridge size.

"Ned was shot with a 0.303? Isn't that the same as Wanda?"

"Yes, it appears so."

I decided I couldn't tell her that I owned the gun. Now it was a possible weapon in two murders, and both victims were my patients. If I said anything about the Lee-Enfield I would be arrested immediately.

"Same killer." I shook my head. Debbie looked at me with cold eyes. I sensed that she saw me as the killer and was sickened that she had to let me go.

"Possibly," she said. "We'll be in touch with you."

Debbie stayed seated. I rose slowly, unsure of what to do.

The chair legs squeaked as I pushed back the chair, and my footsteps echoed as I walked out of the room.

When I got outside, I called Sheila to pick me up.

I could feel the screws tightening. I realized I had to find out who was killing my patients.

17

I sat on the curb in front of the sheriff's detachment underneath Old Glory whipping in the autumn wind. A steady stream of cars passed by, heading to the town's first Walmart that had recently opened. Sheila pulled up in her Malibu just after eleven-thirty, showing me a coffee cup through the window. I got inside and she passed me the coffee.

"I thought you probably hadn't eaten." She passed me a paper bag containing a warm breakfast sandwich with bacon. I was starving. I took a big bite and followed it up with a glug of hot coffee that burned my tongue.

Sheila took a loud sip of her triple triple and put her cup back in the holder, inside an old cup. Sheila was a put-together person, except for her car. Fast food wrappers filled the backseat wells, mud was streaked across the seat, loose keys filled cup holders, old paper cups and plastic bottles were jammed in side door pockets. The inside smelled ripe, like an orange had rolled under the seat and rotted.

"I canceled your day," she said. "Didn't think you'd be up for it. Everyone was okay with that. Except the new guy."

"Doug?"

"Yeah, him. He seemed disappointed."

That wasn't unusual. Doug had just started treatment, and it was common early on for patients to develop a feeling of dependency on their therapist. Missing a session wouldn't necessarily be a setback. It could teach him to tolerate his emotions on his own without a therapist guiding him.

"And Ned was scheduled as well. But."

"You've already heard?"

"Two murders in a week in a town that hasn't had one since Randy killed Jimmy Getson? Yeah, lips are moving around here."

I wondered how much to tell Sheila. She was with me for part of last night, so the sheriff's department would probably interview her to get a sense of my state of mind before I went to Ned's place.

"I'm pretty sure that the sheriff thinks I did it."

Sheila choked on her coffee. After she stopped coughing, she said, "I thought they took you in to ask about him as his psychiatrist."

"I've seen enough of these situations. They're just starting to build their case now."

"Lordie, lordie." I thought Sheila was about to make the sign of the cross, which was odd since she was a self-proclaimed atheist. "I mean, really?"

"I was at Ned's last night. They have video of me leaving his place on surveillance camera."

"Of course Ned would have cameras." She paused. "But if they caught you on camera, wouldn't there be someone else on camera too?"

"That's what I'm wondering. If I was the last one on the camera, and had a motive, they would be arresting me."

"What motive would you have?"

I drank more coffee and decided I would tell Sheila as much as I told Debbie.

"Well, when I went there yesterday, Ned and I had an altercation."

"About what?"

"I'd rather not get into specifics. It's embarrassing. But it got physical."

"And you told them about this?"

"I did."

"Have they questioned anyone else?"

"Not as far as I know. And they didn't arrest me. Something must not be adding up for them yet. But I get the feeling that I'm the one they want."

She huffed. "Don't take this the wrong way, but I just need to hear it from you. Did you?"

"No, Sheila, of course not."

"I just wanted to be clear so that I have no doubts."

I respected that. Sheila trusted me at my word and I trusted hers. If she had doubts, I preferred she ask directly than secretly question my honesty.

"I have to find out who did this. I think it has something to do with me. I mean, both victims were my patients." I left out the part about the missing Lee-Enfield and the 0.303-diameter bullets. I figured there was no good reason to cast doubt on Sheila's trust in me.

"Wanda had a lot of enemies, sweetheart. And Ned too; he was not a nice man."

"You shouldn't speak ill of the dead, Sheila."

"Oh, don't you go getting superstitious with me. Just 'cause someone's dead doesn't make them a saint."

"Sounds like you're the enemy. Maybe I should suspect you," I joked.

"Honey, if I didn't kill my ex-husband, then I don't think I have it in me."

I took another few bites of my breakfast sandwich as we pulled out of the parking lot onto the road. Sheila was biting her thumbnail, and I sensed she was drifting off.

"What's on your mind?" I said.

"I saw Randy yesterday. For coffee."

"Mr. Jesus?"

"You stop that, he's a good boy. But he was different, not so airy-fairy. Like, more real, more like himself."

Keeping up the evangelical preacher act would be exhausting. Eventually, his true self was bound to break through.

"He was telling me that Buddy Getson had been driving by his place a few times. You know, rolling by, slowing down when he passed the apartment."

"Like he was casing the place?"

"More like intimidating him. At least that's the effect it had on Randy. He was scared."

"I thought they were friends. Forgiven and all that."

"Buddy doesn't forgive," Sheila said. "None of that family ever does. They don't say sorry either."

"What are you saying?"

"Buddy Getson has a lot of reasons to hate the Flynns. Randy killed his father, he was pimping Wanda. And I've no doubt that Buddy has killed before. And Ned...well, Ned could've snooped too much."

I decided not to bring up my debt with Buddy. Would he have stolen my gun just to frame me for these murders over a hundred and thirty thousand dollars in debt? Even for Buddy, that seemed petty.

"Randy thinks this?"

"I believe he thinks Buddy had something to do with Wanda's death, yeah."

"He said this?"

"No," Sheila said. "I just get that feeling."

In one of his rants, I could remember that Ned had talked about seeing Buddy and Barrington outside of Wanda's house. Had he seen too much?

"Sheila, I need you to take me to Buddy's place."

She laughed out loud.

"You don't want nothing to do with that boy. He's badness."

"I don't have a choice. I can handle this."

"You haven't dealt with a guy like this..." She stopped herself. "Well, at least not when you had something at stake."

I'd dealt with psychopaths. Lots of them. I could handle myself around them. But Sheila was wrong; I'd almost lost everything because of a psychopath.

We took Hebb Road, an old, partly paved highway through farmland, to get to Buddy's place. It was once the main road connecting the village of Chelsea with Bridgetown. But since the two-lane expressway was built, it was now used by kids on dirt bikes and farmers driving tractors. Dilapidated barns alternated every acre or so with modern farms with bright red and silver livestock shelters and machine sheds.

We passed a strawberry farm and crested a hill before seeing Buddy's place. It sat across from an old-fashioned gas station with analog pumps. The convenience store advertised ginger ale, night crawlers, and trout worms.

Buddy's house was a single-story ranch, immaculately painted forest green and connected to a small greenhouse on the right side. Surrounding the house were bare blueberry bushes of countless varieties, ranging from tart pie-making berries to the sweetest types in existence. Past the bushes was a fenced-in cemetery with half a dozen headstones.

Buddy ran one of the most well-known organic blueberry U-Picks in Maine and had recently expanded into haskap berries. He was a millennial hipster's wet dream. Buddy farmed the land, trapped animals, hunted game, and raised pigs and chickens. He even grew and dried his own tobacco. But the guy also ran a criminal syndicate that spanned three counties.

Sheila parked on the shoulder twenty yards from his mailbox. I could tell she didn't want to get too close to his house in case he saw her with me. I got out, making my way down the sloping driveway. To my left side were a hundred yards of concord grape vines. Their sweet smell filled the air. On Sundays in the fall, ladies from the Presbyterian church flocked here to pick the grapes to make jelly.

The barn door was open ahead, so I headed there. As I approached, Buddy's two Chesapeake Bay Retrievers began barking savagely. They were tethered to a cable beside the house and ran back and forth like lunatics. I took a wide birth around them and entered the barn.

One wall was covered with hanging tobacco leaves in various stages of drying. Next to them hung snares, traps, nets, and cages. On the opposite side was a work bench with a table saw and standing drill. In the middle of the barn, a dismantled, teal 1980s Dodge Ram sat on blocks.

Buddy stood beside his work bench, twisting what looked like a car pipe into a vise. He glared at me before returning to his work.

"You here with your money?" He put on safety goggles and grabbed an angle grinder.

"I'm not here for that."

Buddy put on earmuffs and flicked on the grinder. He buzzed the metal piece in the vise, sending sparks spraying.

After a minute, he turned off the grinder and blew on the metal, shavings sprinkling onto the floor.

"You still here? Without money, we don't talk."

He kept checking the piece of metal, picking at the edges with his gloved hand.

I needed information from Buddy, so I decided to play ball. I pulled out my wallet and made a production of removing all my cash. I counted it out on the tool bench.

"A hundred eighty-five." I showed him my empty wallet. "You've cleared me out for today."

He took off his gloves and put his goggles on top of his head, then scooped up the money and stuffed it into his shirt pocket.

"It's not the money, you know?" Buddy said, unwinding the vise. "I don't need money. I can live off this land for next to nothin'."

He pointed at the farm. "I get fifteen tons of berries an acre, sell fourteen, keep one for myself for winter. I trap year-round, hunt pheasant and deer in the fall. Got potatoes in the back and the pond behind here is full of rainbow trout. I don't need the money."

"You know how to survive."

"Yes, I do."

"Your old man teach you how to do all that?"

"Pffft. Jimmy was a lazy piece of... Couldn't grow a beanstalk. No, over there." He pointed at the cemetery. "Richard James Getson, my grandpa. He lies there watching me. Taught me how to live independently. He gave me this place."

I tried to understand what it would be like to have your grandfather's tombstone facing you day in, day out.

"Jimmy was nothing but trouble. Probably deserved what he got."

Buddy grabbed the metal pipe, walked over to the Dodge, and lifted the hood.

"But I inherited the farm from Richard and then the business from Jimmy. Gotta take the bad with the good."

Buddy reached into the engine, felt around, and then started twisting something.

"So, I'm in the business. And if I start forgiving debts like yours and word gets out, then what?"

He leaned forward, his whole upper body hovering over the engine. I felt an impulse to slam the hood on him. He looked back at me, and I realized he was waiting for an answer.

"Other people stop paying you too."

He turned around and sat on the bumper, tapping the pipe in his palm.

"I don't give a crap about the money, Gus. I'd give the whole business away. But it ain't like there's shares to sell. If I forgive debts, that shows weakness. I show weakness..." He shrugged.

I never thought of Buddy as anything but a low-life criminal. But he was right; the second he let up, someone else would come knocking. Call it a hostile takeover. But even so, even if he could reasonably justify his crimes as a form of self-preservation, he still trafficked pills, women, cigarettes, and loan sharked.

"Did Wanda owe you money?"

Buddy smiled, his sideburns flaring like a fish's gills.

"What's it like being on the other side of the law?"

Silence. I could hear the wind hiss as it hit the side of the barn.

"C'mon, Doc. Word travels fast around here. I hear your patients are droppin' like flies and the sheriff's snare is tightening around you."

Buddy knew. Of course he did. He probably had an ear in the sheriff's department.

"What do you know, Buddy?"

"Just that two of your patients are dead in two days. And that you were the last one at Ned's last night. And it don't look good."

"You know what doesn't look good, Buddy?" I stepped forward, towering over him. "The man who killed your dad gets out of prison, then his sister ends up dead. And the man who saw you and Joe Barrington at her place gets killed. And then Randy sees you driving by his place."

"You don't know what you're talking about."

"Really? Those are facts. And we know you're capable of it."

Buddy crossed his arms. "No one is happier than me that Jimmy got killed. I'd buy Randy a beer to be honest. He did the world a favor."

"But you have to keep people thinking you're in charge and that no one can screw with Buddy Getson and get away with it."

Buddy pounced forward and shoved me in the chest with both hands. The blow sent me back three steps, but I managed to keep my balance.

"Including you. You addict. I didn't kill anyone. So shut your mouth. Are you sure you didn't do it, Gus?"

I nodded.

"Well, me too."

Buddy stomped over to the vise and squeezed it around the pipe again.

"So don't come back until you have my money."

He put on his goggles and ear protection and flicked on the angle grinder, clearly done talking to me. I stepped backward, out of the barn. As I turned the corner, the grinding stopped.

"You weren't the only person there."

"What did you say?"

"I saw you yesterday, on the road, speeding. I was going to follow you and demand my cash. Then I saw you pull into Night Hawk's place. I didn't follow you in. I knew better than to go into that nut's property."

"You saw Ned?"

"No. I kept driving."

"Who else was there?"

"My money."

I stepped forward and twisted Buddy's collar, but he just grinned. "If someone else was there, then they might have seen something."

"I just saw someone we know by the junkyard."

"Who?"

Buddy grabbed my hand and released my grip on his collar. "Money."

18

Buddy Getson's plan to blackmail me with the information that another person was near Ned's place the night of his murder was almost perfect. However, it had one flaw: Buddy did a poor job disguising the person's identity. Because I knew a person who roamed backcountry roads day in, day out, digging through people's trash.

I decided not to tell Sheila about my new lead. It was something that I needed to pursue on my own. Filling her in would only raise more questions about my gambling debt to Buddy, and I didn't want to tell her about that. Bringing up that part of my past would only sow doubt about my honesty. Even though I'd moved on from my days of high-stakes gambling, and was fairly certain Sheila would understand, I didn't want to risk it. I had her trust, and at this time, I needed someone on my side.

"You were right," I said as I slid back into the passenger seat. "Useless."

"Mmm hmm," she said. "Do you want lunch?"

"Thanks, but if I could just get you to drop me off at home. I'm beat. And I've got to check on Anna."

Sheila pulled back onto the old highway. The ride was

mostly silent, giving me time to reflect. I realized how exhausted
I was. I had been pushing myself on adrenaline the past few
days and it was bound to catch up with me. My back was aching.
I hadn't taken my medication again.

I wished I had the courage to tell Sheila everything,
including my missing gun and memory lapses. I felt like each
omission put distance between us. As though with each lie I was
drifting further and further away. But there was too much to
explain, and doing so was to risk her giving up on me.

Sheila left me at the edge of my driveway. I went directly
inside, got Anna on her leash, and let her relieve herself. Then I
left her inside, hopped in my truck, and tore back up the gravel
road.

Wes was a well-known figure in town. People generally kept a
wide berth except when they were dropping off the essentials of life.
Once a week the Rotary Club dropped off a week's worth of frozen
lasagna, casseroles, and dessert. Three times a year the Catholic
Church donated a box of clothing so that Wes could stay warm.

He lived in a leaning shack of a house but had enough firewood for the year, also donated. That left him his entire welfare
check to buy whatever else he needed, which ended up being
tobacco, mainly.

Wes had chronic schizophrenia of the most severe type.
Thirty years ago someone like him would have lived in an insti-
tution. But in the eighties, the importance of liberty overtook
safety, and institutions were emptied. Mentally ill people were
dumped onto the streets to fend for themselves. Most ended up
addicted to crack or heroin, or in prison. Or both.

So, in a way, Wes could consider himself lucky.

He lived in a fantasy world. His mother also had schizophrenia, and he was severely neglected from birth. As a result he was
emotionally stuck in infancy. This meant that his internal world

was still at a preverbal stage of his development, so I could never truly understand it. I once asked Wes to paint his representation of the world. He came back the next session with a canvas covered in dirt and mud.

Some things were too abstract for me to understand.

I loosely knew Wes's favorite junkyard-hunting spots, and given that it was fall and the trees were almost bare, he would be visible from the road. So I decided to systematically drive through the county roads until I found him.

The problem was that even if Wes had been near Ned's and saw everything that transpired, he would be a completely unreliable witness. But if he could identify who else he saw there, I could at least tell Ernie. It would be a start.

After two and a half hours of driving, I saw Wes at Zinck's Auto Salvage. The attendant let me in. I drove through the rows of dented cars and trucks missing doors or hoods or windshields. Mounds of tires and rims lay behind the vehicles. The yard had previously been owned by Ernie Weagle, before he became sheriff and sold it to the Zinck family.

I saw Wes through the trees wearing his favorite dirty overalls and flannel shirt. He had a thick, tangled beard that reached his eyes and he was wearing an old trucker hat. A cloud of cigar smoke surrounded him. He was rummaging through a pile of scrap metal, methodically throwing pieces side to side as though homing in on a specific find.

I parked about twenty yards behind him and hopped out. As I got closer, through the sound of the crashing metal I realized Wes was humming a song.

Find him, find him
Put him in a cage
Smash his fingers
Throw him down the drain

I approached slowly, trying to get in his sight line. But Wes was too focused on what he was doing to notice me.

Until he wakes up terrified
Buried in his grave.

"Wes, hi," I said gently.

He looked up and stared at me, took a few puffs on his cigar, and then got back to work.

Doctor, Doctor, gimme the goods
I got a bad case of it
No pill's gonna cure me now

"Wes, I'm sorry to bug you, but I need your help."

"You need my help?" His voice was shrill on the word "help," and it made my skin crawl.

"Yes," I said.

Wes stopped what he was doing and propped one foot up on a rusty car engine. He put one elbow on his knee and his chin in his hand in an exaggerated attentive pose.

"Someone told me that you were at Ned's last night."

"Night Hawk Ned," Wes said, holding up his finger. "Ned's dead." He nodded.

"Yes, Ned was murdered yesterday. You know that? You were there?"

"Ned's dead. I was not there. Not there, not in my underwear."

"How do you know he died?"

"What's that?" He turned his head abruptly away from me. Wes was attending to an auditory hallucination. "No, the doctor didn't. Doctor didn't kill him." Wes then turned to me.

"Wes, were you there?"

"Not there, not me."

"Wes, listen to me, I need you to focus. Someone killed Ned yesterday, the same person that I believe killed Wanda Flynn."

"Ned died?" Wes began crying, then turned and spoke as

though someone were behind him. "Wanda, Ned's dead. Don't cry, Wanda."

"Wes, are you talking to Wanda?"

"Wanda says 'shut up.'"

I knew Wes was taking his medication because a nurse gave him an injectable antipsychotic once a month. But Wes was more disorganized than I had ever seen him, which made me suspicious that he had witnessed something stressful. And now that he was having hallucinations of Wanda, it made me think that he may have heard her name spoken.

"Did you hear Wanda say something?" I said.

"I hear with my ears. My ears."

"What did you hear, Wes? What did you hear?"

Wes stared at me and took a big haul on the cigar, sending a cloud of smoke in my face.

She will keep on riding

It was starting to get dark. I was getting nowhere with Wes.

The ol' yellow bus in the dark

"What, what did you say?"

Wes looked at me, his expression blank.

And the station pumps out the good ol' oldies

"Did you say yellow bus?"

And she runs from the yellow bus with me

"Ned? Did Ned tell you about the yellow bus?"

Wes didn't answer. He got back to sifting through scrap metal.

But he gave me a lead. It was enough for me.

Ten minutes later I was parked a mile back from Ned's property. He owned about four acres and his house was built in the dead center of his land, the maximum distance from any neighbors.

The police would be searching his home, bagging evidence, and scouring the property, at least during daylight. I knew the school bus was parked on the far corner of his lot. So while the investigators might have been on the property, I doubted they had the manpower to monitor its entirety.

I walked through the woods, the sun low and its rays shining orange light through the trees. I saw the school bus ahead, leaning against a bush like it wasn't sure if it wanted to lie on its side or not. Its front wheels were missing. Yellow grass grew around it, tall enough to reach the top of the back wheels and poke out from under the hood. It would be easy for the police to have a quick look and then dismiss the bus as mere junk, destined for Zinck's.

I waited in the bushes, observing to ensure no police were nearby before walking toward the bus. The windshield was cracked in three places, and the wipers were missing. The bus leaned on its side, but because it was missing the front wheels it also tilted toward the nose. I had to step in carefully in order for it to not tip over altogether.

Inside, the seats were torn and looked like they had been chewed up by squirrels. Mud and dust caked the inside.

I searched up and down the aisle. I looked around the driver's cab and then underneath seats for the safe that Ned described, but I didn't see anything. I stepped out and examined the outside for anything resembling a safe. As I explored, I came across a steel box on the bottom of the bus. It was attached to the frame inside the rear bumper, beside the exhaust pipe. I tried to budge it, but it was welded in place.

I returned to the bus and walked to the rear, bracing myself with the seat backs to get up the incline. When I got there, I crouched down and pulled back the floor, finding a dial for a combination safe.

I regretted not having written down the combination after

Ned had told me. I took a few deep breaths to calm myself and slow my heart rate. If I was relaxed, my memory would return more easily.

The numbers flashed in my mind, but they were just a bit too blurry to see. As though they were obscured by a thin fog. I waited for it to dissipate.

Newton.

I twisted the dial, expecting it to click open, but nothing happened. It was too easy.

Ned wouldn't risk something that straightforward. Anyone who spent more than ten minutes with him would have heard that he expected the world to end in 2060, as Isaac Newton had predicted.

I smiled as I tried it again backward.

The safe opened. It was getting dark and hard to see, so I used the flashlight on my phone. As I pulled out the contents and laid them out on the floor, it was immediately clear that the safe contained more than just information about Wanda's murder. There were old receipts, loose papers with Ned's scrawling handwriting across them, newspaper clippings, and ticket stubs.

He had a map of Zinck's Auto Salvage with crosses drawn in several spots. There was a theory circulated by a few people in town that the bodies of several missing people were buried underneath the auto salvage. The rumor was especially juicy because the business used to be owned by Ernie Weagle.

I found a picture of Wanda grinning at the camera. It looked like an old graduation photo.

A flash of blue light caught my peripheral vision. I looked out the side window and saw a light bobbing through the bushes toward me. I immediately turned off my phone's light. On the silhouette I could make out a belt and weapon.

Combined with the police-grade flashlight, I knew it must have
been someone from the sheriff's department.

I began packing Ned's materials so that I could review them
at home. I was collecting them into a pile when I noticed something on one of the crumpled pieces of paper. I unfolded it and
smoothed it on the floor, letting my eyes adjust to the darkness.
It was handwritten.

Doug Steele - seen with Wanda - not his real name

The blue light shined at the window. I tried to quickly pick
up the papers, but half of them slipped out of the pile and fell to
the floor.

"Hey, who's there?"

I looked out the window. The officer was thirty yards away.

I pressed the latch for the side window and pushed, but it
would only open halfway. I squeezed through, hanging onto the
remaining stack of papers as I pushed with my hands to get my
hips through. The flashlight was on me now, so I gave a final
thrust and popped myself out of the window.

I fell six feet, dropping the papers, and they fluttered away in
the breeze.

I heard the officer's footsteps pounding around the bus, so I
sprinted into the woods, racing past trees and over branches. I
ran until the flashlight was far enough away that it looked like a
firefly, and then I walked back to my truck.

I nearly lost my footing stepping into my truck, and banged my
shin painfully against the running board. I got myself inside,
stretching the seatbelt across my lap as I pulled away. I startled
at the sound of cars being crushed at the junkyard. I drove onto
the old highway and along the shoulder, then parked in a field
in front of an old, collapsed barn. I pulled out the pack of ciga-

rettes I'd shared with Renee, lit one up, and leaned back against the headrest.

Doug. Ned suspected Doug. Ned lived with a sickness inside his brain that affected his perception and his ability to separate fact from fiction. It locked him inside his own little world. All of us are trapped inside of what we perceive, or at least what we allow ourselves to sense. And I was no exception.

Was I simply seeing what I wanted to? But he wrote Doug's name. What about him? Maybe it was just another loose thought, unanchored by any foundation, that floated around an insane man's mind. Maybe he wrote the name because it was the next thing on the conveyor belt of conspiracy theories in his head.

I wanted Doug there, at Ned's. If Doug was there, it meant I wasn't the only person who saw Ned. Doug was a grieving father, but maybe he just played the part. My first reaction when I saw him was that he was a psychopath.

But a killer? That would be sick. Anyone was capable of murder, though. That darkness was in all of us. We kept the beast tamed, but with the right circumstances the lock pins could align. And the monster would be unleashed.

I thought about calling Debbie Parks and telling her Ned suspected that Doug killed Wanda. But my words would lack context. I had as much chance of getting Debbie to tap dance to a show tune as I did of getting her to follow up on a rambling man's suspicions.

But even if I had something more concrete that placed Doug at Ned's place the night of his murder, I couldn't in good conscience go to the sheriff. I still owed Doug a duty of secrecy, and that duty held unless I thought there was reason to suspect he would kill someone else. Calling Debbie with nothing but a name seemed desperate and would do little to prove my innocence. I was scared.

My cigarette had burned down to the filter, so I tossed it out the window and pulled back onto the road. The sky was turning neon pink as the sun descended. I drove through town, and by the time I passed the Irvine gas station I had to turn on my headlights. Night came quickly at this time of year.

I didn't have a clear plan forward, but I decided to call Sheila with my next step. She picked up and asked me where I was.

"Just going out for a drive."

"Driving where?"

"Through town." I decided not to tell Sheila anything more. I didn't want to pull her in until I had more information. "Could you give me Doug's address?"

"Doug Steele? The patient?"

"Yes."

Sheila must have sensed something in my tone, because she didn't ask any questions and gave me the address.

"Thanks. Goodnight." I was about to hang up when Sheila spoke.

"Gus. Be careful."

I hesitated ending the call. I wanted to tell Sheila what I found in Ned's safe, but it felt too flimsy to bring up and risk my relationship with Doug. I decided to deal with it on my own and find out more information before throwing around half-baked theories. At least Sheila knew where I was going.

After a five-minute drive, I pulled up to Doug's place, a thirty-foot trailer dropped on a patch of gravel in an area of cleared woodland. There was no deck or outdoor chairs. A few rusty propane tanks leaned against one side. The curtains were pulled tight on the two front windows, and the house was dark.

I kept the car running with the headlights pointed at the house as I approached the door. A couple of cars raced past on the road. After they left, it fell quiet.

I wasn't sure what I would say if Doug opened the door. I hadn't thought that far ahead. I couldn't expect him to admit to being at Ned's. But if I talked to him, I might be able to draw the truth out of him.

I opened the screen door and knocked a few times, waited a minute, then gave another series of knocks. Nothing. I pressed my face to the glass to try and see through the quarter-inch gap between the window frame and curtain but could only make out the corner of a couch.

I tried to turn the doorknob but it was locked. I was creeping toward the back when a call blared through the speakers on my truck's Bluetooth, shattering the rural quiet.

I rushed over to my truck and pressed talk on my steering wheel.

"Well, finally." It was Renee. I glanced at my phone in the cup holder. Six missed calls.

"Sorry." I opened the door and jumped into the driver's seat. "Running a bit late."

"It's okay. Karen is here." Karen. I winced at her name. I almost missed her. And I invited Renee over at the same time.

"Shoot, I am sorry."

"No," Renee said. "It's so nice that you invited me to meet your daughter. And we are having a great time. Isn't that right, Kay?"

I heard Karen's voice in the distance. "Hi, Dad."

19

I managed to race to my cabin in under thirty minutes without skidding off the road or getting caught by a cop. Two cars were in the driveway. I recognized Renee's electric-blue Golf and assumed the other belonged to Karen, so I parked on the side of the road to avoid blocking them. I stayed in my truck for a few minutes, pondering how I would explain being late for what would be the most important dinner date I'd had in years.

I got out and walked toward my house. I could hear Waylon Jennings's "Luckenbach, Texas" on my record player.

This was the first time I'd seen Karen in three years. And I nearly botched it. Karen wouldn't tolerate any excuses from me. She'd heard enough.

Karen had been poisoned by her mother to hate me. And I didn't exactly help the situation. When Karen was twelve, I promised her Princeton as long as she got straight As and overcame her fear of public speaking. She held up her end of the bargain; she never got less than an A+, and she played Annie in the school musical. I knew I could save the money through my work as an expert witness.

I had been up three hundred and fifty grand. If I'd walked

away she could've gone to Princeton twice. I carried the guilt of that decision like a cross on my shoulders. Every month that I sent her money in those unmarked envelopes, it was as though I was slowly repaying my debt to her. But her opportunity had already passed.

Part of me wondered whether she came because of money. Either to take the cash she'd accumulated and throw it in my face or ask me for more. I secretly resented that our relationship had been whittled down to nothing but a series of financial transactions that flowed only one way.

What stung most was that she blamed me for the breakdown of my marriage. I'd strayed on one occasion with Karen's nanny. Her mother told Karen all about it, and made a production of firing the nanny Karen had grown to love. I couldn't bring myself to tell Karen that Meg was already deep into her affair at the time of my indiscretions. After that I played longer rounds of Blackjack and poker. The stakes got higher and higher until I'd squandered her college fund. I tried to explain, but she never bothered to listen to my side of the story. I wasn't sure she would understand, anyway.

I had a lot to cover in this meeting with Karen, but mostly I just wanted to hold my baby again.

I walked around the cabin to the patio door and stepped inside, surprised by what I saw. Renee was at the stove, turning meat over in a sizzling pan. Karen was next to her chopping lettuce and cucumber. Both talked, their backs to me, while swaying to Waylon's gritty baritone. Even Anna didn't notice me. She was lying at the edge of the kitchen, watching them.

Renee was the first to turn.

"Gus!" She ran over and gave me a kiss on the cheek. I'd been wanting to kiss her, and she'd managed to do it in such a nonchalant manner that it seemed like we were already living together.

"We were hoping to have dinner all ready by the time you got here. You must be tired. Let me get you a drink."

As Renee returned to the kitchen, Karen slowly approached me. She'd changed. Her blonde hair was chopped into a bob and dyed light purple. In big block letters across the front of her T-shirt was the phrase "I run on feminism." I'd picked her name, after psychoanalyst Karen Horney, who famously challenged Freud's idea that women's psychology revolved around their yearning to have a pecker. Horney retaliated by saying that women were relegated to being baby breeders by a patriarchal culture of men who overcompensated for their feelings of inferiority because they could never bear children. She called it womb envy. Take that, Sigmund.

I smiled, relieved Karen was at least standing in front of me, but she didn't smile back. She fiddled with the bottom hem of her shirt, as I remember her doing when she was uncertain. I thought about stretching my arms out for a hug, but I felt like it would be too much of a risk.

"I missed you," I said. Her eyes twitched at that, and she looked around the dining room like she didn't hear me. My hope of a quick "let bygones be bygones" dissipated.

"Neat place you've got here. Rustic."

Karen had become a city girl. The idea of chopping down trees, baiting hooks, and wearing clothes that smelled like campfire disgusted her. Her mother had trained her to love nature and protect the environment the way only a city dweller who lived in a thirty-story monstrosity could. I wondered if Karen even remembered gutting walleye with me when she was ten.

"Minus the burned-out wing."

She at least laughed at that. "Like I said, rustic."

There was a pregnant pause, and I realized I was staring at her. Karen was beautiful, and she stood with such confidence, shoulders back and squarely facing me. There wasn't an ounce of that tentativeness I remembered.

"Long drive down?"

"It was good. I needed a drive."

"Are you on business?"

She snorted a laugh. "Not a lot of work out here, Dad."

I couldn't tell if that was meant as a dig at me. Her dream was to make a difference on a global scale. The clear path to doing that was through an Ivy League school, but I'd torched that possibility. But she paved her own way, from a tier-two university and then working her way up to an NGO.

"What brought you out here?" Part of me was getting suspicious as to why she would announce that she was coming after all these years.

She looked at me blankly, as though I should know. "Well, I thought that-"

"Drinks!" Renee popped up next to Karen with a bourbon and Coke for me, and wine for Karen. She winked at Karen as she handed her the glass. "Gus, you have the most beautiful daughter. She reminds me of mine."

Renee toasted and the three of us clinked glasses. I muttered some cliché about reunions and Renee invited us to sit down as though it were her place. She brought over three plates, placing a plate of braised venison with roasted potatoes and salad in front of me.

"Wait, let me take a picture of you two," Renee said.

I looked at Karen, who seemed to shift nervously at the idea. "How about we do a selfie of the three of us?" I offered, as though that would somehow make it less awkward.

Karen came over and stood a couple of inches from me. Renee put her arms around me and leaned her head on my shoulder. I held up my phone and snapped the picture. I looked at the photo and thought about asking Renee to take one of me and Karen, but Karen had already taken her seat and I didn't want to push things.

"How did you get in? I'm pretty sure I locked the place," I said.

"Are you sure?" Renee said, reminding me of my faulty memory.

"Renee figured it out," Karen said.

"Paving stone," Renee said, covering her mouth with her hand as she was mid-bite.

I was struck by how comfortable Renee was making herself. I wanted to be alone with Karen, but Renee clearly wasn't going anywhere.

"It's so nice of you to have invited me to meet your daughter," Renee said. "She is an absolutely amazing soul. You must be so proud."

"Very proud."

Karen looked down and took a bite of cherry tomato. No meat on her plate. She'd been a vegetarian since she was fifteen in protest of animal rights violations.

"You don't eat meat?" Renee said.

"Vegetarian."

"You might want to think about it, Gus. Given..." She winked at Karen.

"Given what?"

"Oh, nothing," Renee said, and ran her hand down my neck. "Girl stuff."

"Dad, I'm happy you found someone. I am."

Renee grabbed my hand and squeezed. We had hit it off, but I wasn't even sure Renee and I were an item. But she and Karen seemed to get along and I needed dinner to go well, so I decided to let it go.

"I'm glad I came," Karen said. "To be honest, I just needed to hear that from you. And when I got that in the mail..." She shrugged.

I felt heaviness in my chest as she mentioned the monthly envelope. I always wondered if they reached her. But I wanted Karen to come because of me, not my money.

"I've been sending you envelopes every month."

"Those don't matter to me. It's not what I'm talking about."

"They don't matter?"

"No."

I bit down on my lower lip, telling myself to let it slide. "It seemed to matter when you decided to stop speaking to me."

"Money?" Her demeanor changed. "Money."

Renee began shaking and wheezing and pointing at her throat. She made a little squealing sound. She was choking, so I got up and tapped her on her back, initially softly, then harder until she began coughing. I rubbed her back as she slowly raised her head and looked at Karen and then me.

"I'm so sorry, this is just embarrassing." Renee covered her face.

"Not at all, can I get you some water?"

"I'm okay." She wiped her eyes. "I should let you two talk."

Both Karen and I insisted she stay. I suspected that Karen also sensed the two of us were careening toward an argument and needed Renee as a buffer.

"Let me just go for a walk for a couple of minutes to come back to myself."

I sat back down with Karen in uncomfortable silence. I wanted a relationship with her so badly but not if it was based on money.

Renee suddenly returned and sheepishly put up her hand.

"Um, Gus?"

"Yes. Everything okay?"

"There's a man outside. Says he's your patient and that he needs an appointment... now."

———————

Doug arriving at my home was a major boundary violation. Sessions happened in the therapy room, nowhere else. Maintaining that boundary was an absolute. Patients needed to learn to tolerate their feelings between sessions. I'd crossed the line with Ned, and I wasn't about to do the same with Doug.

I stepped outside and walked down the steps. It was dark except for a rectangle of light shining from the kitchen window. Doug paced in a row of my Honey Crisp apple trees, kicking at the ground with every other step. The shaky cigarette he held to his mouth glowed as he took a drag.

"I know I'm not supposed to be here," Doug said, looking at the cigarette between his fingers. "But I didn't know where else to go."

I wasn't sure if his arrival was an attention-seeking ploy to work out some unconscious abandonment issue, but he was distressed. And he looked scared.

"I wouldn't have come, but you canceled today." He took a long drag and sniffled at the same time. "This just couldn't wait."

"What's going on, Doug?"

Doug put his hand over his face and began crying.

"I don't know if I can."

"You've come this far."

"I can't, no." He began to walk toward the road. "I'm sorry."

He staggered as he made his way up the driveway. I realized he was drunk. I wanted to let him go, but the thought of Ned suspecting Doug made me reconsider.

"Doug, wait." I caught up with him. "You came here to talk about something."

Doug puffed out his cheeks and tapped his foot on the ground. I could smell whiskey on his breath.

"Been drinking?"

"A little."

Therapy was next to useless when people were intoxicated. Genuine emotions couldn't be accessed. But secrets could still be spilled.

"You come to my home, Doug, you've been drinking, you're a wreck. There's something you need to tell me. Something you need to get off your chest."

"I can't."

"You wouldn't have come here if you didn't trust me."

Doug took deep breaths.

"Whatever it is that made you come here, if you don't bring it up then it will haunt you until you address it."

"You speaking from experience?"

"Excuse me?"

"You haunted by something?"

I shook my head in confusion.

"Doug, I'm here for you," I said. "Not for anyone else. And especially not to air my issues out."

"You're good at keeping secrets."

I wasn't sure if that was a question or a statement. But if Wes was right and had seen Doug at Ned's, then I needed to know.

"I'm the best."

"You don't tell?"

"I don't."

Doug took another long haul on his cigarette and suddenly looked calm.

"Okay," Doug said. "I couldn't let it slide. I just couldn't."

"Let what slide?"

"What he done to that woman."

"Which woman?"

"Wanda."

I took a step forward. "Are you saying you know who killed Wanda?"

"He admitted it."

"Who are you talking about? Ned?"

Doug nodded and stared at me with intense eyes. "He admitted what he done. Just before." Doug wiped his nose. "You know what? I don't regret it."

I was unsure of what to say. Doug had killed Ned. I felt a glimmer of vindication. But the idea that Ned killed Wanda didn't sit right with me.

"You knew Wanda?"

"I met her a few days ago at this bar. Gorgeous woman." I remembered Wanda telling me about a man she met while waiting for Joe Barrington. "She was tellin' me about some man stalking her. Driving by. Scaring her. Then she ends up dead. Police aren't finding anything, so I started looking around and I find the guy she was complaining about. I knew he was your patient, so I followed you. I went in there and found him. I saw he had the same gun they say killed Wanda. He admitted it. So."

"You shot him?"

"With the gun."

It wasn't me, I thought. Doug was a disturbed man, and my initial impression that he was a psychopath might have been correct. But if Ned had killed Wanda, then maybe he was justified.

"You couldn't let another one go," I said, back on autopilot, a therapist linking the present with the past. "The way you let Maddie go."

Doug's face seemed to melt into sobs and he crouched down, propping himself up with his arm.

"I never told you the truth," Doug said. "The truth about

Maddie." I directed him to sit on a long birch log at the edge of my driveway.

"Tell me the truth."

"She was a good girl. Always listened. Would do anything I asked of her. Had a smile that-" He sighed. "She dreamed big. Bigger than I could imagine. Bigger than I could provide. I made mistakes."

"We all make mistakes with our daughters."

"She got older, you know, and then she started testing. Testing the limits. My ex, she couldn't handle it, but me, I tried to roll with it. But she kept pushing and I couldn't let her. So I was... I'd clamp down." His voice got huskier. "Maybe too hard."

"But it all changed when she met this boy." Doug's eyes shot back and forth. "He was bad news. He tells her to challenge us, to push back. And she falls deeper and deeper. More trouble. And I can't control her anymore. I tell her she has to respect the rules or she's out. Next day, she runs away."

Doug looked out in the distance and lit another cigarette.

"She didn't die of a drug overdose. That boy killed her." Doug stood up. "He took her from me and he killed her." He grabbed a boulder and heaved it onto the road. "My baby girl!" Doug stumbled into a ditch, crying.

I stepped down into the ditch and helped him up. Doug collapsed in my arms, sobbing.

"I couldn't let it happen again. I couldn't."

If Ned had killed Wanda, Doug would see her as his daughter. And unbelievable rage would have come out.

"I won't do it again. It just hurts so bad."

"It's over, Doug. It's okay."

He breathed heavily, trying to gather himself. "I just needed to get it out."

"Sunlight is the best disinfectant."

"Have you ever kept a secret like this?"

I had. I wanted to tell Doug that my silence could end up implicating me in the murders. But my oath had to stand. Doug wasn't going to kill anyone else, and I could rehabilitate him. I had to trust that the investigation would eventually clear me of any wrongdoing.

"Your secret is safe."

"Thank you. I'll go now."

"Do you need a ride, Doug?"

"I need to walk this off. Jimmy Beam got the better of me tonight." Doug turned around. "You know, I just wish I could have killed that guy who killed Maddie. I wish I strangled that Robert."

I stood in the dark, mentally running through my altercation with Ned. The evidence was all there—his obsession with Wanda, the pictures, the necklace. I just didn't want to believe it.

Doug had disappeared into the darkness. Something about his words struck me. Robert. A wave of realization washed over me. Maddie. Overbearing parents. A runaway. A creek. I'd heard this story before.

Robert had been my patient.

———

"I called you because there are some things I need to tell you before I go," Robert said.

Doug found a chair by the window, dragged it beside the bed, and sat down. The gun dug into the small of his back. He didn't say anything. He had to let the man speak. He needed to know.

"You think I know something. You wonder where she is?" Robert coughed dryly. "What matters is that she's away from you."

"Where is she?"

"First tell me why?"

"Why what?"

"*The beatings. Chaining her up. Keeping her prisoner, drugging her?*"

Robert had taken Maddie away and now had the audacity to question his authority. He ignored the gifts, the hugs, everything that he did for her. It was as though all of that didn't count.

If she hadn't met this boy, she wouldn't have defied. He had set simple rules, straightforward to understand, and if she didn't obey then there were consequences. By disobeying, she chose those punishments.

"*You don't understand.*"

"*I do. Because I read about psychopaths. You wanted to control her, she was yours, your possession, your little robot.*"

"*She was free.*"

"*And the second she didn't act like a machine, you beat the shit out of her. You took everything from her,*" Robert said. "*Hollowed her from the inside out.*"

Doug shook his head. He'd loved her, cared for her since she was an infant. He was shaping her, sculpting her into what he knew was a good person. Some might not agree with the method, but she knew the rules and respected them until she met Robert.

"*Don't try to disagree. You wanted to keep her as a child so that she was defenseless and totally dependent on you. Even if she wanted to leave, even if she wanted to run, she feared you.*"

Doug felt a shaking in his chest. The boy looked frail, yet had the energy to judge him, as though he knew him.

"*She hated you.*"

Doug reached behind his back and felt the butt of the gun.

"*Are you sure you want to do that before I tell you where your daughter is?*"

20

I stood at the patio door, listening to the pattering of waves against the rocks as I stared through the glass. Renee was at the sink washing dishes. Karen stood beside her with a tea towel, drying plates and examining each before putting it in the cupboard. They were chatting and then looked at each other and laughed, their heads cocked back in almost perfect synchronization. It was a scene of two women in my life becoming closer, connecting. Me on the outside looking in. I'd been there before.

I opened the door and stepped inside. Renee looked at me and turned off the tap with her elbow.

"Boy, talk about taking your work home with you." She laughed. "He seemed distraught."

"He was," I said. "But everything's okay."

Renee's hair fell over her face as she dried her hands with a towel. She swept it back and retied it in a ponytail as Karen put away the last few plates.

"We left your plate out."

"Thanks, but I'm not hungry right now."

I felt nauseous. Doug had said the name Robert, that much

was certain. And I believed that the Robert he was referring to was a former patient. If so, Doug wandering into my practice and paying for ten sessions up front was beyond coincidence. I wondered if my mind was making connections that didn't exist.

"Okay." Renee handed me my bourbon and Coke as she sat down at the kitchen table and directed Karen to sit across from me. Renee was nearly vibrating with giddiness, but I stayed flat, finding it impossible to stop thinking about Doug. "Karen's got news she wants to share."

Karen smiled coyly and took a deep breath.

"I'm pregnant."

Renee clapped her hands and then hugged Karen from across the table. My mind was still catching up to what Karen had said when Renee and Karen raised their glasses.

"What did you say?"

"I'm pregnant, Dad."

Renee slid my glass into my hand and raised my arm until our three glasses clinked.

"How... how far along?"

"About four months."

I squeezed my eyes tight and tried shifting my mind to the present. I feigned a smile.

"Who?"

"Is the father?" Karen said, and then crinkled her nose. "Donor."

"There's no father?"

"That's kind of how it works," Renee cut in.

Karen nodded. At age twenty-three, she decided to get donor sperm to have a child. I couldn't help but think about what sort of oedipal complex the kid would have.

"I want a child, Dad. I'm ready."

"Are you sure about this?"

"Yeah." She let out a nervous laugh.

"But you're so... How are you going to?"

"I'm glad you're so worried about me."

"Karen, how will you raise the child. How will you afford-"

"I can figure it out. I have a lot of support. Mom said-"

"You haven't finished school. You're-"

"Whose fault is that?" Karen said coldly. "I thought you'd be at least a little bit happy for me."

I reminded myself that I wanted a relationship with my daughter.

"I am. I am. It's just that I worry about you."

I thought of Doug clamping down on his daughter. I tried to let go.

"I wasn't going to tell you. I wasn't," Karen said, wiping tears from her eyes. "And then I got that last envelope from you." She smiled. "I thought we could start over."

Something broke inside me. The envelope. I wanted her to use the money. I wanted to help. She was telling me that money was what brought her back to me. She cut me out because of money, and now she was back for the same reason.

"A handout," I said.

Renee put her hand on my forearm.

"Excuse me?"

"You want your money. That's why you're here."

"No, I don't, I-"

"Over three years I don't hear from you because of money. My fault. I blame myself every day. I try to make it up. And now you're coming to get what's yours."

Tears streamed down her face, and she looked like I'd just taken the wind out of her.

"You're an asshole. No wonder Mom left."

Karen picked up her glass, put it in the sink, and left. On her way out, she tossed an envelope on the table.

Renee's hand was pressed to her temple. She shook her head.

I downed my bourbon and leaned my head against my hands.

"Okay." Renee spoke slowly. Her lips moved but words didn't immediately form. "That was harsh. But recoverable. You guys have some talking to do."

I didn't say anything. I told myself I hadn't ruined my chance at reconciliation. She had.

"I think I can smooth things over with her. I know where she's staying."

I looked at the envelope. Was any money left inside? I reached for it, but Renee took it from me.

"You calm down, leave this for later. I'll come back in the morning."

I grabbed my keys, ran to the basement, and turned on the lights, then unlocked file cabinet after file cabinet in search of Robert Fisk's file. I knew it was there and had to consult it to refresh my memory. I rifled through the file cabinets containing my yellow notebooks. When I reached the F section, his file wasn't there.

I decided to look for his blue shadow file in the file cabinets across the basement. Eventually I found a notebook with the initials R.F. It was thin. I'd only seen him once, six years ago.

I took it upstairs and sat at the kitchen table. I read my handwritten notes from our meeting, the memory of the story he told me seeping back in.

Robert came in with the common "I'm not here for me, I'm here for a friend." It was a common refrain I heard from young men too embarrassed to admit they had an emotional problem.

The difference was that Robert truly came for advice on how to help a friend.

Robert was twenty-two when he came to see me. He presented as a confident and stable young man. He was articulate and made solid eye contact as we spoke. When he was eight, his father died of cancer. That's when his mother packed them up and bought a place in rural New Hampshire.

Their property backed onto a creek, and he would go out fishing on his own. He was quite the angler too. He described that he held the state record for brook trout, coming in at just a hair over nine pounds. In late summer, the creek would dry out, and as the water levels fell, he would venture further downstream looking for deeper pools to fish. One day, about three miles away, he saw a girl around his age, alone and barefoot, on the other side. The second she spotted him she ran away, off into the woods.

After that, every summer, once or twice, he would have a sighting of the blonde girl. One time, he tried to speak to her. She froze up, turned, and ran back into the forest, but she came back the next week. They initially spoke a few words, and eventually, she told him her name.

Madeline.

Robert described her as childlike, behaving much younger than her age. She was homeschooled and had no friends, although she talked about a cousin visiting her occasionally. As time passed, she began asking him more questions about his life. It became apparent to Robert that she lived a very sheltered existence.

As he became a teenager, his feelings of intrigue developed into romantic feelings for Madeline. Gradually, they had longer visits at the creek, but she would never cross over to his side or let him wade over to hers. He found this odd, but was also excited by the idea of a forbidden love.

One day, Robert was able to convince her to come over to his side of the creek. He described her as stiff and shaking as she crossed, terrified by the idea. She spent all of ten seconds on his side of the creek before scurrying back over. She cried hysterically that her parents would see that her dress was wet at the bottom and that she had walked off their property. She ran into the woods and he didn't see her again for an entire year.

Robert kept walking up the creek at least once per day, hoping to see Madeline again.

And he did. One evening during spring, when the water was high, he saw a figure pop up from the creek, gasping for air. He ran over, jumped in, and pulled Madeline from the current. She was unconscious but began coughing up water as they reached the creek's edge. They lay on the grass together.

Robert began asking her how she fell into the water and she confided in him that she was trying to kill herself. As he probed further, she described in horrifying detail the abuse she suffered from her parents. She was never allowed off the property. Her father noticed the day she got her dress wet, so she was shackled to a floor anchor in her room for three months. Once the snow fell, she was unchained, but her parents took away her shoes, as they figured she wouldn't be able to run away barefoot. When her father learned that she had been talking to a boy over the creek, he beat her with a tire iron until she was unconscious. If she ever questioned her parents' decisions, she was promptly given sedatives and restricted from eating for days to ensure her submission.

I listened as Robert listed abuse after abuse that Madeline had suffered over years. He had begged her to go to the police, to run away with him, but she firmly refused. And he was reluctant to do so without her agreement.

By the time he finished, we were already an hour over time.

He wanted advice on what to do to help Madeline out of such a horrific situation.

She was effectively trapped by fear—fear of retribution if she were to leave them, and fear of the scary unknown world that her parents created for her. And over time, she would be trained to sympathize with her parents. She would think that they were only doing their best. That their treatment of her was reasonable because she was "bad." That the world was against them and they were in it together. It was Stockholm syndrome, a spell she was under that gave all power to her abusers and left her utterly powerless, so much so that she wasn't even able to end her own life. She was left completely alone.

And that spell would last until someone like Robert came along to pop it.

In effect, Robert wanted to kidnap her. But the reality was, abusers who exerted this level of control over people wouldn't stop under any circumstances.

I had contemplated reporting the situation to the police myself, but that was complicated by a few factors. First, Madeline was over eighteen. While I could call authorities, the courts had ruled that mandatory reporting of abuse was limited to children. Second, I didn't know her full name. I thought that the best course of action would be to discuss the situation further with Robert at our next session, but he never showed up. And when I tried to call him, I realized he had given me a fake number. I ultimately decided not to pursue it further and keep Robert's dilemma to myself.

I put down the notebook. If Madeline was, in fact, Maddie, Doug's daughter, then Doug and I had a connection that was beyond coincidence.

What bothered me was that Doug said Robert killed his daughter. I began regretting my decision to not pursue Robert and Madeline. I wasn't sure I could bear another patient killing someone on my watch.

I went upstairs and opened my laptop to search for Robert's name. Unsurprisingly, no Robert Fisks around his age in New Hampshire, Vermont, or New York readily came up. He had likely given me a fake name.

I tried numerous variations of his name, checked school graduations, but I was unable to find a lead. After forty-five minutes of searching, I was ready to give up.

I scanned my notes again, hoping for some sort of clue. I looked at the wood stove and then my fly rod leaning against the wall. I stared at the rod, my eyes running from the thin tip down to the cork handle as though I was searching for something. I finally realized why.

"Fishing."

I ran up to my laptop and Googled "New Hampshire record brook trout." After a few pages of searching I found the name of the person who currently held the record: Robert Di Santis.

I kept on my search and typed in "Robert Di Santis New Hampshire."

The second entry from the top was an obituary.

The picture was Robert. I scanned through the obituary quickly. It said that fourteen months ago he had died "after a prolonged illness." Doug had mentioned that Madeline had gone missing years earlier. If Robert had killed her, there would have been an investigation.

I looked up Madeline's name along with the last name Steele, New Hampshire, missing.

Did you mean Madeline Boone New Hampshire

I clicked on the link and it refreshed the search. There were two pages of articles on Madeline Boone. I clicked on the first. "Father not giving up search for Madeline Boone." The photo was of Doug—real name Kurt Steele—discussing how his daughter had disappeared years earlier and he had been searching for her ever since.

"For years, we met there by the creek. I was her only contact to the outside world. She was so naïve. You kept her that way."

Robert pointed to the mug with a straw on the table next to him. Kurt hesitated and then lifted the mug to Robert's mouth, waiting as he took a labored sip. Kurt pictured smashing the mug on Robert's face, moaning as blood splattered across the bed. That would have to wait. He needed information first.

"As we talked, she got more and more depressed. Just sad. She heard about my life, my mom, and what being loved was like. And you'd just about destroyed all the life inside of her."

"Where did you take her?"

"She begged me, she begged me to let her go. She was afraid to run away because of what you would do to her if you found her. But she couldn't stand being there anymore. Maybe I shouldn't have told her about what normal parents were like. Kept her ignorant."

"Where is Maddie?" Kurt said, his voice shaking. He breathed heavily through his nose. He needed to see her again.

"She wanted it. Because she wasn't living. And she was afraid to leave. She was stuck and there was no way out. And there wasn't."

Robert's mouth opened and closed, as though the words couldn't come out.

"I even asked a shrink. He said the same thing. You'd never stop." Robert pressed his tongue against the inside of his teeth and shrugged. "I had to."

"Had to what?"

"She wanted to die, Mr. Boone."

Kurt rubbed his hands together, not fully comprehending.

"I told her I'd give her a kiss. And when she came close, I put my hands around her and..." Robert nodded.

"You killed my Maddie?"

Robert turned slowly, looked Kurt in the eye, and smiled. "After that, I rowed out to the middle of the lake with her body and left her there."

Kurt stood up and grabbed the gun from his belt. He pushed it against Robert's temple. "You piece of shit, how could you kill an innocent girl?"

"You made me do it."

21

In the basement I took my Remington 7600 pump action out of the safe along with eight rounds and put it in my sheepskin zipper case. It was light and my most reliable gun. I grabbed my tool bag and threw in a flashlight, headlamp, pry bar, adjustable screwdriver, hammer, and a handful of wrenches.

I went to my truck, threw the tools and my rifle in the back seat, then drove in the dark toward Doug's trailer. I took an old road that hugged the Persey River. The rapids were loud with the recent rainfall rushing downhill. The currents ate away at the river bank.

I turned north and followed the road that circumvented the town, past the saw mill and boat storage yard. The moon was hidden by clouds and the sky was totally black. I left my headlights off. I worried that as a possible suspect in the murders, the sheriff's department could be trailing me. Staying inconspicuous on the roads was critical.

I could picture Doug killing Ned, holding the muzzle inches from Ned's head, squeezing the trigger, and walking off like nothing happened. Debbie said I was the last person on camera, so I wondered how Doug managed to get inside Ned's house without being seen.

I thought about Doug's daughter. It wasn't uncommon for children in these situations to identify with their parents and see them as only wanting the best for their children. Or seeing their parents as victims against the dangerous wider world. I'd worked with a sixteen-year-old victim of incest who insisted for two years that it was her fault for what she viewed as tempting her father. Only when in a group therapy session another teenager called her dad "a messed-up psycho" did something click and she realize her innocence.

I drove past Doug's trailer without slowing down, but I was able to see that no car was parked out front. I drove a quarter mile further and parked my truck off the road under a dripping pine tree. I grabbed my tool bag and rifle and walked into the woods between my truck and Doug's trailer, which appeared empty. Doug had walked home from my cabin, and there was a real possibility he was passed out in a ditch somewhere, so I figured I had a solid head start on him. It would give me time to get inside the trailer, look around, and leave before he arrived.

The trailer and its surroundings were completely dark. Part of the trailer's vinyl siding had slipped out and was bouncing in the breeze. I walked up the steps and unscrewed the light bulb over the door, then knocked. After a few seconds I tried twisting the door knob, and when that didn't work, I hit my shoulder against the door. The dead bolt refused to budge.

I'd lived in one of these trailers when I first moved to Bridgetown and was having my place built. On more than one occasion I had locked myself out.

I walked to the back of the trailer and found a seven-gallon pail full of rainwater. I dumped it out and then stood underneath the bathroom window, leaning my shotgun against the wall and dropping my tool bag on the grass. I switched on the headlamp, grabbed the pry bar from the tool bag, and stood on top of the pail, then shoved the end of the pry bar between the frame and window. I rocked it back and forth, gradually increasing pressure until the interior plastic latch snapped off and I was able to slide the window open.

I pulled myself up onto my elbows and slid through the narrow window, tipping head first into an empty bathtub. I knelt, peeled the slimy shower curtain off my face, and stepped out of the tub.

A razor, deodorant, and Calvin Klein cologne were on the sink ledge. I opened the medicine cabinet but found it empty. I left the bathroom and moved into a narrow hallway, flicking on my headlamp. I turned right, into the bedroom. A mattress without a bed frame lay directly on the floor with a mess of blankets on top. Cigarettes were piled in an ashtray on the nightstand.

I opened each dresser drawer and swept through T-shirts, socks, and underwear. Besides learning that Doug was a Hanes man, I found nothing of importance.

I left the bedroom and moved through the hallway into the kitchen. Pots, plates, glasses, old pop bottles, and pizza boxes littered the countertop. The stove was covered in grease and the garbage bin was overstuffed. I opened cutlery drawers, cabinets, and rummaged through random jars of keys and coins.

I came across a locked drawer. I gave it a few good jerks, but it wouldn't budge. I tried several keys from the jar, but none of them fit. I'd found nothing in the trailer that would link Doug to Ned, or even Robert.

I walked into the bathroom and picked up the pry bar from the bottom of the tub. I then moved back to the kitchen, placed the end of the pry bar into the gap between the drawer face and cabinet, and rocked it until the drawer front cracked and splintered. I wiggled the drawer off and placed it on the floor.

Inside I found an open box of photographs and an eleven-by-fourteen hardcover scrapbook.

I picked up the photographs and leafed through them, looking at Doug and who I assumed was his daughter at various ages: Doug holding her as an infant in the hospital, pushing her on a swing, eating birthday cake. I took the photo of her as a teenager standing on the shores of a lake and stuffed it into my pocket.

I lifted the scrapbook, made some room on the counter, and then put it down. I quickly flipped through the pages. They were filled with writing from front to back, some sort of journal. I began leafing through more slowly and stopped at an entry. My fingers trembled as I scanned the page.

Gustav Young DOB November 2, 1963

Harvard Medicine class of '87

North Eastern Institute of Psychoanalysis - left in 2016/17 - dismissed due to gambling addiction

Investigated in 2015 by College of Physicians

Married Meghan Siegel, divorced 2016

Schedule:

My schedule was scribbled in calendar format over months. It outlined my office hours, the times I went fishing and hunting. It included when I went for dinner in Bangor with an old colleague, when I went to visit my mother in the home. It had itinerary-level details of my spring vacation to Vienna.

I flipped the pages frantically. Newspaper clippings and photographs were glued to some of the pages. Other pages were dedicated to my musical and food preferences. The information spanned fifty pages. One of my annual evaluations from the institute was stapled to the next page, with a phrase highlighted and circled:

Excellent Memory - superb integration of information

The next five pages were about Sheila Gustafson, her divorce, her home address, her hobbies and friends.

There were ten pages on Wanda. Details about the men who visited, her relationship with Joe, the bars she frequented, newspaper columns written about her testimony in Randy's trial.

I flipped the page.

Karen Young

I scanned down. Doug had compiled information about Karen. He outlined her academic history, he had her address, he knew jogging routes. I scanned to the bottom. My stomach felt hollow.

Pregnant.

Footsteps on the front stairs. Keys jangled. I shut off my headlamp, closed the notebook and put it in the drawer, and tried to press the drawer front back on. I glided to the bathroom as the front door opened and keys dropped onto the counter.

I stepped into the bathtub, grabbed onto the window frame, and pulled myself up. My foot slipped and knocked a bottle of shampoo off the edge, sending it rattling into the tub.

"Who's there?" It was Doug.

I scrambled out of the window, flipping over and landing hard on my knees. Footsteps pounded through the house and the front door squeaked open. I got to my feet and limped toward the woods, fifty feet away.

I made it to the edge of the woods as a flashlight swept across me.

"Hey you!"

I didn't turn around. I just kept running into the woods. The flashlight approached as I ran deeper and deeper into the forest, stumbling over roots and dead fall. As I turned hard left, my footing gave way and I rolled down a hill, coming to a stop beside a fallen pine.

I looked up. The light was flashing at the top of the hill, so

Doug hadn't spotted me yet. I slid underneath the pine branches so that I was mostly obscured and tried to catch my breath. Only then did I realize I left the gun by Doug's trailer.

Light appeared, methodically scanning left to right, then up and down and back again. Boots ground against the rocky hillside. Branches popped and cracked nearby. In the dark I had trouble locating the sound.

"Where are you?"

I held my breath, trying to stay motionless. I reached for my cell phone, but had a second thought. Even the slightest bit of light could be seen in this dark.

I heard a car engine. Bright light illuminated the forest at the top of the hill. Then I heard the footsteps recede and a car door open and shut.

I slid out from under the tree and checked my phone. No service. There was another hill ahead with a small clearing where I hoped to connect to a tower. I plodded up the hill, holding my phone high until I saw two bars. I dialed Renee's number.

"Renee, it's me. Are you with Karen?"

"Yes, but—" There was static on the receiver. She came back on and whispered, "I'm not sure she wants to talk to you right now."

"That's okay, I can't blame her."

"Gus? Gus, you're-cut-ing-out."

I backed up a few steps. "Better now?"

"Better."

"I need you to take Karen somewhere out of town. I think she's in danger."

"In d--ger?"

"Yes, take her to a hotel in Portland. I will meet you there as soon as I can."

The call dropped. I tried to call back, but it wouldn't connect. I had to hope that Renee heard my message.

I walked in circles at the top of the hill, holding my phone up until one bar appeared, then dialed Debbie Parks's number.

"Hello, Deputy Parks here."

"It's Gus Young."

"Oh." There was silence, and I couldn't tell if I was losing the connection.

"Are you there?"

"I'm here."

"Debbie, I'm going to give you a name. You need to look into him for the murder of Ned Gamble."

Silence.

"Are you there?"

"Are you saying that you think you know who killed Mr. Gamble?"

"Yes."

"And how do you know that?"

I promised Doug secrecy, but only with the understanding that no one else was at risk. Seeing the notebook changed things. Although Karen seemed safe with Renee, I couldn't be sure.

"He told me."

"Someone confessed to you?"

"Yes."

My phone buzzed twice with a message from Sheila.

Sheriff on his way to your house. They have a search warrant.

I stared at the screen. That explained the distance in Debbie's voice. All evidence pointed to me, and at the final hour I was calling to tell them that a patient of mine confessed to the murder. I couldn't blame her for her skepticism.

"Where are you now, Gus?"

I began wondering what surveillance capabilities Debbie

and Ernie had. If I stayed on the line, would they eventually be able to track me down? If they found me, I would be placed in a holding cell; it could be hours or days before I was questioned. And Karen would still be out there.

"I can't tell you right now."

"Gus, I need to-"

"Kurt Boone. He killed Wanda and Ned. He's coming for me. You need to find him."

I hung up.

Kurt couldn't let Robert die peacefully. He'd taken that away from Maddie.

He pressed Robert's neck against the mattress and held the gun to his head.

He heard a metallic click behind him and turned around.

Robert's mother stood fifteen feet away, the barrel of a shotgun pointed at him.

"Let my boy die the way God wants it."

Kurt squeezed the gun grip, leaving his finger touching the trigger. He wanted to look Robert in the eye as life drained from him the way Robert had done to Maddie. Robert had turned her against him. Robert had destroyed everything Kurt had worked so hard to create. They had molded Madeline to be just the way they wanted, but Robert shattered it all.

But the boy would die anyway. Kurt had seen his own mother die of cancer, writhing in pain until the very last moment. Shooting him would be merciful. It would only ease Robert's suffering. The boy didn't deserve that.

Kurt released his grip on Robert's neck and raised his hands as he turned around.

"You can put that gun there on that nightstand," she said, keeping the shotgun pointed at him. "Go on."

Kurt spit on Robert's face before placing the gun down. He adjusted his jacket and swept his arms down his sleeves before walking out of the room. He took several steps down the hall before something that Robert said struck him. He paused before turning around.

"I just want to know one thing. A shrink told you something?"

22

As soon as I got back to my truck, I connected my phone to the Bluetooth. I hadn't figured out a plan on how to find Doug, but I knew what I had to do next. I punched in the number and let it dial as I pulled back onto the road.

Sheila answered my call and immediately asked whether I had received her text message about the search warrant.

"Yeah, I saw it. Thanks for the heads up."

"Where are you now?"

"I'd rather not give specifics. But I know who killed Ned. Doug did."

"The new guy?"

"Yup. I think he killed Wanda too. I think both murders were because he was trying to frame me."

"Why on earth would he do that?"

"I'm not sure. But he is connected to a former patient of mine."

"How did you find that out?"

"He came to my house while I was having dinner. He told me that a man named Robert killed his daughter. The name stuck with me so I found it in a file." I explained how I had broken into Doug's trailer and found the detailed journal about me.

"What did the sheriff say?"

"I told them Doug confessed to killing Ned. But I don't think they believed me. I think they're convinced I had something to do with it."

"Ernie will hear you out. He's a good man."

"I think we're past that point, Sheila."

The sheriffs would see the gun safe and the rounds matching the Lee-Enfield in my basement. That, along with surveillance footage, would be more than enough to arrest me. I needed evidence to link Doug to the murders.

"I need a favor."

"Shoot."

"Robert Di Santis died about a year ago. I found an obituary online. I need to find his next of kin. And I can't go home right now."

As I drove past the Irvine, I checked my gas tank and saw that I had enough for another hundred miles.

"Spell the name."

I spelled it and said, "I think he lived in upstate New York or New Hampshire."

Sheila hummed into the phone. "Got it, I think."

I swerved onto the shoulder and pulled a pen from the cupholder. I couldn't find a piece of paper, so I grabbed an empty paper coffee cup and wrote on the side of it.

"There's a Jina Di Santis in Vermont. Jina is spelled with a J, just like the obituary." She read out the phone number and address.

"That's great."

"You think she's the one?"

"I'll try."

I switched to the other line, and once the phone began ringing, I merged Sheila onto the call. "Stay quiet," I said.

A woman answered.

"Hi. I'm looking for Robert Di Santis."

A smoker's throat cleared. "I'm sorry. He died a while ago."

Click.

"I'd say we have a match," Sheila said. "I guess that's your next stop?"

"Yes," I said, making a U-turn and heading toward the highway for Vermont. I estimated the drive would take two and a half hours if I gunned it.

"Sheila, Doug had notes on both you and Karen. I sent Karen along with Renee."

"That woman you've been seeing?"

I paused. I hadn't told Sheila anything about Renee.

"Word gets around, Gus. But by all accounts she's a lovely lady. Even the quilting ladies are fond of her."

"I'm just getting to know her. But I sent her to a hotel near Portland with Karen. I want you to go and meet them there. I'm not sure it's safe in-"

"I think I can handle my-"

"Please, Sheila. Just until I get back."

"Okay. Sure."

I read her Renee's number. "And Sheila, they don't know anything about this. So can you keep it quiet?"

"My specialty."

Newport was half an hour inside Vermont's state lines, and Jina Di Santis's house was another fifteen minutes further. As I crossed New Hampshire and entered Vermont, the rain started. The radio had been warning that the remnants of the Carolina hurricane were heading north. The wind picked up and shook my truck, so I had to grip the wheel with two hands. As the rain fell harder, I turned my wipers all the way up.

Another call came through. It was Ernie Weagle.

"Hi, Gus. Just following up on your call with Deputy Parks."

"I thought you were busy searching my house." I paused, but he stayed silent. "Thought someone from your office would've told me."

"The warrant wasn't signed off when she spoke to you. But they're at your place now. Listen, I went to talk to Mr. Steele."

I said nothing. I wanted him to speak.

"He has an alibi. I was able to check it out."

"For Ned?"

"Actually, he has one for both murders," he said. "I just wanted to let you know. Courtesy."

"Thanks." I hung up and pressed my palms into the steering wheel.

Ten minutes later, I was driving up a winding byway to Jina Di Santis's house. It was quaint and had a cottage feel, with a couple of neatly trimmed birches growing on the front lawn next to a decorative well. The rain was coming down in sheets, slapping against the grass. I realized that Jina Di Santis wasn't going to just let me in. I was a stranger showing up at her place unannounced at midnight during a storm. Even country hospitality had its limits.

I got out of the truck, and before I reached the front door, I was already dripping wet. Faint light was coming from the window. I made it to the front door, rain beating against my head and back.

There was no answer when I knocked, so I hammered on the door again. I thought I heard footsteps inside.

"Mrs. Di Santis, if you're in there, I just need to talk to you."

Rain pounded the ground like a snare drum.

"I need to talk to you. I am not here to hurt you. My name is Gus Young, I'm a psychiatrist and I knew-"

The porch light turned on and the door opened.

"Wet night." A woman who looked to be in her late fifties

stood behind the open door. Her hair was in rollers and she wore a beige housecoat. She still had mascara on, and blush on her cheeks. She struck me as one of those ladies who didn't go outside after washing her hair because she thought she'd get a cold.

"Jina Di Santis?" I said.

"That's me."

"My name is Gus Young. I knew your son Robert."

She nodded. "I always wondered if you'd show up. Come in."

I walked into the house and took off my shoes. The place was so clean it sparkled. The carpets in the living room looked freshly cleaned and the vinyl floors in the entryway shimmered. Cinnamon lingered in the air. A cross was fixed on the entryway wall and a print of Da Vinci's "Last Supper" hung over the dining room table. She led me through a hallway past the kitchen and into a sunroom with windows facing the forest in the back.

She pointed me to the microfiber sofa with a crocheted throw over the backrest. Hooked rugs hung everywhere. A fire crackled inside the wood stove. A collection of plates and vases were lined up on a shelf next to it.

"Would you like a tea or water, Doctor?"

"I'm fine, thank you."

She left the room and returned holding a frame. She flipped it around and showed me Robert's graduation photo.

"Handsome boy, don't you think?"

I smiled. "It's how I remember him."

"A very nice boy. Always helping."

"You must miss him."

"Oh, very much so." She smiled in a detached way, as though she only partly meant it.

"How did he die?"

"Leukemia." She took a sip of tea. "Non-Hodgkin's. The bad kind."

"Was he sick for long?"

"Many months. He sort of... wasted away. There wasn't much the doctors could do."

"Do you have other children?"

She shook her head. "Only Robert."

Jina had the sort of distant approach to grief I saw infrequently. Either in denial, or so religious that she saw death as a blessing, as though it truly wasn't goodbye, only "see you later." I noted three crosses on my way in, so my money was on the latter option.

"Where is he buried?"

She shook her head. "He's not." She pointed toward the plates on the wall. Between the decorative vases was a porcelain jar that I realized was an urn.

"I wasn't able to part with it yet. So it stays. So when people come, you know."

I didn't exactly know. But I assumed she meant that if people wanted to pay their respects to a bowl of ashes they could.

"You said that you wondered if I would come by?"

"Well, that man kept coming back, three times I think, after Robert died. Wanting to know who you were."

"Who I was?"

She nodded.

"Was his name Kurt?"

"Kurt Boone, yes."

"Boone."

"Yes."

"Did he say why he wanted to talk to me?"

"He wasn't the sort of person I wanted to have much of a conversation with. I assumed it was something to do with what he and Robert talked about before he died."

"Wait. Kurt Boone was here with Robert?"

"Oh yes. Robert was insistent that he meet Mr. Boone before he died."

"Robert invited him? How come?"

She shrugged. "They spoke in private."

"You know nothing?"

She gave me a sympathetic look. "Robert valued his privacy."

"Oh come on, Jina. Robert insists on meeting Mr. Boone and then Boone comes back after Robert dies looking for me? And you don't ask any questions?"

"I'm so sorry, Doctor. Robert wanted to tell him something. He said he needed to "clear things up" before he died. It's important, at least in my faith, to make peace before the Lord takes you home. I just assumed Mr. Boone wanted to ask you questions."

"About what?"

She shrugged.

"About what happened to his daughter?"

She looked at me doe-eyed, as though she knew nothing about it.

"Oh you can knock off the act, Jina. Boone told me that Robert killed his daughter. That's why he called Boone, isn't it? And somehow Boone got my name out of this."

She shook her head slowly. "Robert would never hurt anyone." Her nostrils flared. "And when did you talk to Mr. Boone?"

"Long story. Let's just say he killed some people to try to get to me."

Her eyes twitched. "He's killed someone?"

I nodded. "I need to know everything you know about him. He's trying to frame me; I need to understand why."

Jina took a long, deep, stuttering breath and ran her hands

nervously along the sides of the picture frame. "I didn't like that man. For years he kept coming by."

"Here?"

"No, at our ranch in New Hampshire. We had to move because he kept threatening Robert."

"What did he want?"

"He was looking for his daughter. He thought she'd run away. That Robert was hiding her. The man would follow Robert, he'd show up at his school, at his sports games. But Robert just wouldn't call the police. I wanted him to, but he refused. I believe Kurt Boone drove that girl to suicide. His controlling nature. Oh, the things that Robert told me that they did to her. Death would have been a blessing. The beatings he gave. The drugs the mother gave her. She couldn't escape them."

"But why would Boone connect me to this?"

"All I know is that once Robert was gone, Boone blamed you."

I thought about that. Why would Doug blame me if Madeline killed herself?

"Oh, but he wasn't the worst of it." She shook her head. "That woman. Evil. Had that beautiful exterior, and she could charm, but the devil lived inside of her. She came here, smiling, sweet, lovely, wanting to discuss her daughter. And the moment I disagreed with her, poison flew from her mouth. She knew everything about me, told me she'd poison me. And she probably could."

"How so?"

"Well, she was apparently a pharmacist. Had access to all sorts of drugs. I tried to make a complaint about her to the professional body, but she had left the state. If I could just find-"

I was no longer listening to Jina. It was as though her voice faded into nothingness and I was floating. I reached in my pocket, opened my phone, and flicked through the photos until

I found my selfie with Karen and Renee. My hand shook as I turned it to her.

"Is this her?"

Jina stared at the phone for a long moment and then looked at me. "Tori."

Kurt walked up the driveway, heat radiating off the ground, swaying as he processed Madeline's death. Six years of searching and it led to nothing. He knew Madeline wouldn't have willingly left him; she needed him. He knew that the only way she would be gone is if someone had ripped her away.

Before he came here, he'd called her, after more than a year of no contact, to tell her that the boy wanted to meet.

Kurt held the phone, punched in the number, and hesitated before he pressed dial.

She picked up on the second ring.

"She's dead."

"What?"

"He killed her, dumped her in a lake. He made it sound like he did her a favor."

"Did you?"

She wanted him dead. She said Kurt didn't have the guts before, but now was the time.

"He's dying. He's going to go any day."

"You left him?"

"We can't bring her back."

"You let him get away with it! You are weak, weak."

He knew she wouldn't understand. She needed revenge, she needed blood. She had lost control, and needed something to anchor her again.

"You know, Tori, he didn't come up with it on his own."

23

I hit the road back to Bridgetown. The wind gusts made the truck doors shudder, and long pools of rain were collecting on the highway. The ditches were starting to overflow and the trees beside the road were whipping back and forth. Although I wanted to drive full speed, I could only see about twenty feet ahead. And being pulled over by police would slow me down enough to effectively end any chance I had of finding Karen.

I had nine missed calls from Sheila, all during my meeting with Jina Di Santis. She didn't leave any messages, which told me it was about something she didn't want recorded. I called back, but it went to voicemail.

I had a heavy feeling inside me. I'd instructed Sheila to find Karen and Renee, but that put her in danger. My fear was only heightened when she didn't answer.

I thought about messaging her, but I knew that probably wouldn't be useful either. As I crossed the border from New Hampshire into Maine, I decided to try her once more. She answered.

"You're okay," I said before she could speak.

"I wish I could say the same for you, sweetheart."

"What's going on, Sheila?"

"The police issued a warrant for your arrest. They've been by your place. They called me looking for you."

I wasn't surprised. I'd been running on the assumption that the sheriffs were going to link the murder weapon to me.

"They found cartridges that match those at the scene from both Ned and Wanda." She cleared her throat. "They found a pair of deer antlers and Wanda's necklace at your place. I believe you didn't do it. But this isn't good."

I began organizing the pieces together. The fire. The necklace. The gun.

"They've been setting me up, Sheila. For months."

"Who is that?"

"Doug and Renee."

"Excuse me?"

"They're formerly married."

"Tell me more."

"About six years ago I saw a patient. Only once. He wanted help with-"

The wind pushed my truck into a puddle and I started hydroplaning. The water thundered in the wheel well. I gradually turned the steering wheel to nudge the truck back onto firm pavement.

"Sorry," I said after righting the truck. "This patient, Robert, wanted advice on how to help a girl who was being tortured by her parents. They were pathologically controlling, going to sick extremes."

I stopped there, noticing my memory was clear and I was able to easily retrieve information again. I realized that I hadn't taken the pills for my back in a few days.

"Jesus." I smacked the steering wheel. "She was dispensing them."

"Who was?"

"Jina said Renee drugged her daughter to keep her calm. She was dispensing my medication, and the past few months my memory has been failing."

"You think she drugged you somehow?"

"I think so." I continued with my theory about Robert. "So at some point after I saw him, the girl ran away. But the parents were angry. They kept searching for her, wanting her back. And then about a year ago, the boy dies of leukemia. But on his death bed he confesses to the father that he had killed her."

"And the father is Doug?"

"Yes, real name Kurt Boone."

"And Renee?"

"Her real name is Tori."

"And they're married?"

"Jina said she thinks they divorced after Madeline disappeared. But they're working together."

"And this boy, Robert, killed her?"

"No, Jina insists she killed herself."

"Really?"

"I believe her. That boy wouldn't have killed her."

"Hmmm," Sheila said, and then drifted into silence.

"What is it?"

"Well, she doesn't have an obituary. Not one that I could find. If she killed herself-"

My mouth went dry and I chewed on my fingernail as I stared into the dark sky. Sheila was right. People who died by suicide would have obituaries. There had to be an explanation. Perhaps Doug refused an obituary as part of the denial process.

"So what does he have against you?"

"Robert's mom says he blamed me. That after Robert died he kept coming back to find out who I was."

"Blamed you?"

"Apparently they talked about me. Maybe he just couldn't

accept that she died. You know, people with a psychopathic make-up, they can get delusional and maybe-"

"Was there any reason for him to blame you? What did you talk with Robert about?"

"Nothing. I talked to him about Stockholm syndrome. That people like Doug wouldn't stop. They just won't. Not until..."

"Not until what?"

I closed my eyes as the memory of my session with Robert came back and sighed. "I told Robert that people like Doug wouldn't leave him alone, wouldn't stop looking for his daughter until she was dead."

"No," Sheila said forcefully. "You don't do this to yourself."

"But-"

"Don't."

"If I hadn't said that, Sheila-"

"Honey, listen to me, you aren't responsible for what people do. They make their own choices."

I tried to soak in Sheila's words. She was right, from a logical perspective. And I had to focus on finding Karen.

"You think Robert told Doug?"

"He must have. That's the only explanation."

"And Renee?"

"She's Madeline's mother. And by Jina's description a total psychopath."

"And Karen's with her?"

"Yes."

"I'm at the hotel. In the parking lot."

"Sheila, you can't go in there."

"I'm tougher than you think."

"You need to call the police, Sheila. Tell them that they have Karen and are responsible for Ned's and Wanda's murders."

I drove under an overpass and saw a cruiser on the shoulder near the exit ramp. I checked my speed and was well under the limit, but I slowed down anyway to avoid attracting attention. As I passed, I saw an officer illuminated by the glow of a computer. I kept an eye on him in my rear-view mirror, but he didn't look up.

"I think they started the fire in my place to get my gun. One of them shot Wanda, probably Renee, because Doug has an alibi. She then worked her way in with me, all the while Ned was onto them. So they killed Ned too, with the same gun, again linking it to me. Then Doug told me he did it, knowing I'd keep it a secret."

"The necklace?"

"Ned had taken Wanda's necklace when he found her on the road and I took it from him. I'd left it on my truck seat. Renee must have taken it. The antlers, I'm not sure."

"And they knew Wanda?"

I checked all my mirrors again. No police lights.

I recalled Wanda waiting for Barrington in the bar the night before she was killed. She met Doug there, and called Barrington from his phone. "Barrington," I said. "Sheila, tell the police to get Barrington's phone. Wanda called him from Doug's phone the night before she was killed. This links them."

"I see them," Sheila said.

"Doug?"

"Renee and Karen. They're getting into a car. Karen looks happy."

"They haven't hurt her yet. But Doug must know that I was in his place."

"I have to follow. In case we lose them."

"No, Sheila." I shook my head. "Let the cops handle it."

"Gus," Sheila said. "If they slip away, we might never see Karen again."

She was right. I hated the idea of potentially putting Sheila in harm's way. But if we lost sight of Karen, they could head in any direction and my hope of finding her would be over. I knew that even if Sheila got through to Ernie Weagle, explained the story, and cruisers were sent out, Doug and Renee could be two states over by that point.

"Be safe."

A sign said another forty-five miles to Bridgetown, which would take thirty minutes. The rain lashed against the windows, but I sped up, needing every extra minute I could get.

My phone buzzed with a text message from Sheila.

Past Waterloo, up private road, right at T

Five minutes later she sent another one.

Past ATV trail down toward Redway. This is deep woods

I nearly swerved off the road as I read the text. Were they really going there? How did they know where the shack was? But most of all I knew the road was a dead end. They would see Sheila once they stopped.

I dialed Sheila but the phone immediately went to voicemail.

24

The shack that I built where the Persey met the Redway was only three miles from my cabin as the crow flies. In daylight, using the trails I cut, it was less than a thirty-minute walk. But in the dark with torrential rain and needing to bushwhack an alternate route, it could take hours. Doug and Renee would have taken one of the main trails, and I had to assume they were waiting for me.

I couldn't go home, because the sheriffs were looking for me. So I decided to leave my truck on an empty piece of land about half a mile from my cabin. I parked it out of sight behind some overgrown wild blackberry bushes.

I got out of the truck and was immediately stung by the rain pelting my face. I stayed to the side of the mushy dirt road so if I saw headlights I could quickly dart into the bushes.

I neared Herman's home. I decided to walk into his property so I wouldn't have to cross my land and risk being spotted by the sheriffs. Even if they were gone, my firearms would certainly have been seized and I couldn't go to the shack unarmed.

Herman's barn was used for storage and sat at the corner of

his property about ten yards from the woodland edge. I looked up the hill at Herman's main house. No lights were on inside. Herman usually passed out drunk at eight-thirty and didn't get up until daylight. I thought about banging on his door and asking him to call the sheriffs, then thought twice about it because I couldn't be sure they hadn't already told him I was wanted for two murders.

The barn's double doors were padlocked. Rain pooled around the barn, and I could see a spot along the bottom where the boards were rotting. I pressed it and the wood crumbled underneath my thumb. I kicked at the rotten boards until they caved in. I was able to rip off three of them, creating a gap wide enough for me to squeeze inside.

Herman kept dozens of snares and traps hanging against two walls. I searched along the back wall until I found a wooden box holding one of his rifles, an old Remington Model 11. I found three shells and pushed two in the magazine.

Before leaving I pulled out my cell phone and tried to dry it off with an oily rag, then turned it on to find only five percent battery life left. I tried calling Debbie Parks and Ernie Weagle but neither answered.

I finally decided to text Debbie.

Two dead at shack where Redway meets Persey. Active shooter.

I hit send. I hoped my text wouldn't be prophetic, but I needed to get the sheriffs out to the shack as quickly as possible, and a dead body was the most sure-fire way.

I slid out of the barn and moved back into the bushes. Clouds were thick, no stars or moonlight to help direct me. I had to go on memory, and now that I hadn't been taking the medication for a few days, I felt more confident in my abilities to navigate in the dark.

I knew that if they took the main trail from the east, they

wouldn't be able to see me coming from a westerly route down the ravine. That way, I could cross over the Persey and approach the shack from the other side of the river. At this time of year, the current wasn't usually too strong, but the rain made that a wildcard.

The torrential rain didn't let up. My shoes and socks were waterlogged. I tried to wipe the rain away from my eyes. It was cold, just ten degrees above freezing, and I felt pins and needles in my hands. But I had to ignore the pain and press forward.

As I reached the top of the ravine, I thought I heard a thunderclap. Not until I heard a second one a moment later did I realize it was a gunshot.

I dropped down prone into a puddle deep enough to almost entirely submerge my body.

I had the shotgun propped on a fallen branch and pointed into the dark woods. My eyes were already adjusted to the dark, but I could not see the gunman.

But if they were shooting at me, it meant they saw me and would have to speed up their plan. I had to get to the shack as quickly as possible, so I was forced to abandon my plan to cross the river. I no longer had the advantage of surprise.

Two more shots cracked, kicking up water and debris two yards ahead. The rain was so loud that I wouldn't be able to hear footsteps approaching.

I was about fifteen yards from the edge of the riverbank. While lower land was not ideal, it gave me separation from the shooter and offered me a chance to get to the shack.

I hopped to my feet and jumped off the riverbank, landing on an incline ten feet below. My footing gave way and I slipped onto my back, then slid down the side of the bank. I fell into the river and lost my grip on the gun.

The water rushed over me, pulling my face under and threatening to drag me downriver, away from the shack. I scrambled to my feet and my lower back began seizing up. I saw the gun barrel bobbing up and down in the water as it floated away. I threw myself at the gun, my fingers squeezing the tip with just enough pressure to pull it toward me.

I tried to touch down with my feet, but the water was too deep and began dragging me downriver. I quickly swam perpendicular to the current until my foot felt the soft river bottom and I was able to regain my balance. I pulled myself onto the river's edge.

The shack was two hundred yards ahead. My wet clothes flapped in the wind, and the trees beside the riverbank swayed up and down. I took large steps, sloshing through the river's edge.

As I approached the shack, wind whistled and howled against its rickety boards. Three silhouettes moved in front of the shack. I lifted the shotgun, the butt firmly against my shoulder, and took aim.

"Stop there," I yelled.

The figures stopped.

"Don't move."

I walked carefully up the slippery riverbank, keeping the gun pointed at the shack. As I got closer, I saw that the silhouettes belonged to Karen, Sheila, and Renee.

Karen and Sheila stood with their arms bound behind their backs. Rolled-up bandanas were tied over their mouths. Their hair was matted down from the rain, and streaks of blood ran down their faces. Karen tried to scream, but Renee swung her arm and hit her square in the face, sending her to her knees. Sheila winced and whimpered as Renee jerked Karen back to her feet.

"Stop there, Tori," I said, moving forward, gun aimed at her head.

She grabbed Karen by a fistful of hair and dragged her

beside Sheila, then pointed a handgun at Karen's head. Karen recoiled and moaned through the cloth stuffed in her mouth.

"Who first, Gus?" she said. "Your daughter?"

I didn't say anything, only tried to aim the gun at her body, but she wisely stepped behind Karen. I was about eight yards from her, which meant if I shot, the bullet spread would be somewhere between eight and fifteen inches. I'd have to be inch-perfect in order not to hit Karen too.

"You'll know what it's like. To lose what you love most."

"You don't know love, Tori," I said. "You owned Madeline. She was your possession. Yours to control."

"I loved her."

"No, you didn't. You don't know how to love."

"And you do?" she screeched. "Karen hates you. She told me that, Gus. And she will die hating you."

I ignored her and continued. "And then Madeline went and did the one thing you couldn't control," I said. "She took her own life."

Tori screamed again. "No, you told him to kill her. You told him to!"

"I told him you wouldn't stop until she was dead. I was wrong about that."

"You'll know what it's like." She raised the gun and her wrist tensed.

I squeezed the trigger. A shot rang. I felt a punch in my shoulder, like I'd been hit by a boulder, and fell to the ground. I dropped onto a knee and the shotgun fell from my hand. I got on all fours, but when I tried to push myself up a searing pain radiated from my shoulder to my neck. As I righted myself, Doug emerged from the woods, pointing a rifle at me.

He stepped forward, the rifle barrel a few feet from my face. With his free hand, he grabbed my shotgun and tossed it into the woods.

"Good thing I didn't kill you, Doc," he said. "I need you to feel what it's like to have your daughter killed." He stepped backward toward Tori. "You want to do the honors, or shall I?"

"We both know you don't have the guts."

Tori raised the weapon and pointed it at Karen's head. Karen screamed, and I saw Tori look me square in the eye as her hand began to tighten.

I jumped to my feet and lunged at Tori, my hands wrapping around her body.

Bang.

I clattered into her, smashing her against the wall of the shack and onto the ground.

Bang. Bang.

Karen and Sheila screamed.

I looked underneath me. Ragged tissue hung from Tori's throat, and she gurgled as blood spilled from the wound. Still holding the gun, she began turning it toward me. I grabbed her wrist, squeezing until she loosened her grip and the gun fell to the ground.

I grabbed it and turned around. Doug lay on his back, gasping for air like a dying fish.

Karen and Sheila were on their knees, hands behind their backs, scanning the darkness through reddened eyes. I crawled over and put an arm around each of them.

I heard a splashing behind me. I turned and saw the outline of a person approaching from the woods, holding a rifle. The figure stopped twenty yards away and reached into its jacket, then unscrewed a bottle top and knocked some of the contents back before moving forward again. I smiled as much as I could despite the pain.

"Want some?" Herman said, emerging from the darkness and holding out the flask.

"How did you know?"

Herman offered his hand and lifted me up. He pulled a hunting knife from a sheath on his belt and freed the women's hands.

Karen and Sheila ran over and hugged me. I held them close.

Herman examined my shoulder. "I hate to do this, but hold still." He poured his moonshine onto the bullet wound, and I winced at the burning sensation. "I hate to waste good alcohol."

Herman stepped over to Doug, crouched down, and checked for a pulse. He shook his head and then walked over to Renee. He looked at her sideways as he tilted her head.

"Yup," he said. "She's still got those dead eyes."

I released Karen and Sheila from my hug.

"Herman, how did you know?"

"Well, when I see you rippin' my barn apart and runnin' away with my gun, I figured something was up."

"I'll fix those boards for you."

"Damn right you will."

The sheriffs didn't arrive for another forty minutes. At the time of my text, they were still busy scouring the county for me. They hadn't checked their voicemail, so they didn't get Sheila's message until after they arrived at the scene.

Deputy Parks took a brief statement from each of us, then let Herman drive Karen, Sheila, and me to the hospital instead of waiting another forty minutes for an ambulance. I convinced Herman to take my truck, rather than his old beat-up Chevy, mainly because I didn't think his old beater could make it that far. By the time we reached the truck I was hypothermic, numb, and in a daze, which was probably for the best, as I wasn't ready to process what had happened.

I do remember that Karen sat next to me in the back of the truck, at one point leaning her head on my shoulder.

25

I slept until the afternoon, oblivious to the beeps of IVs and heart monitors, the overhead PA, and nurses talking loudly in the chart room. I was in surgery by the next morning, and the surgeon was able to remove the bullet in my shoulder and sew me up in under two hours. They loaded me up with antibiotics and pain killers and sent me to my room.

When I opened my eyes, Karen and Sheila were sitting beside the window playing Crazy Eights. They were both cleaned up and wearing fresh clothes. A couple of get-well-soon cards sat on the windowsill next to a bouquet of daisies.

"Well good afternoon," Sheila said. "How do you feel?"

"Pretty good, they've got me on some good stuff."

"The doctor says that you'll live."

"You sound a bit disappointed about that," I said.

"It was a close one, sweetheart. I wasn't sure."

I laughed out loud, but stopped when my neck and shoulder became sore.

"You were right, you know that?"

"About what?"

"That loon was poisoning you. The doctor did a drug screen. You had barbiturates in your system."

I slowly smiled. "I thought I was losing it."

"You weren't the only one."

Sheila stood beside me and gently pushed my back forward. "You're sitting awkwardly, let me help." She fluffed my pillow and slowly lowered me back into a more comfortable position.

"I shouldn't have ever dragged you into this," I said.

"I dragged myself into it. And you couldn't have done it without me."

"True."

"You know, you told me that being your office manager would be part time."

"Are you asking for a raise, Sheila?"

"I think we should call it danger pay."

I grabbed a Styrofoam cup of ice chips and shook a few into my mouth.

"I'm going to leave you two. Karen, I'm going to bring you some decent coffee from down the street."

Karen smiled as Sheila left. "I like her, Dad."

"She's a good person. Doesn't let me get away with anything."

Karen stood up, holding an envelope. "I picked this up from your place. I found it outside fluttering around."

"The letter?"

She nodded and handed it to me. It was written in hand-writing similar to mine, but must have been sent by Renee or Doug. I finished reading it and looked up at Karen.

"They sure knew how to put what I was feeling into words. I don't think I could've written it better myself."

Karen laughed. "When I first read it, I thought to myself, 'Dad couldn't have written this.' It's too heartfelt."

"I guess dealing with emotions isn't my strong suit. At least not my own."

Karen's hand slid down to mine.

"I haven't been good to you," I said. The words started pouring out as though her touch had opened a valve inside me, one that brought tears to my eyes too. "Too wrapped up in my own head to notice anyone else."

"You had a lot in your head, Dad."

I shook my head. "That's no excuse. My problems shouldn't have become your problems. Good dads don't do that."

Tears welled up in her eyes and dripped down her nose.

"Will you be there for me now?"

I nodded. "And for my grandchild too."

I was released from the hospital the next day. Wanda's funeral was held at the Catholic church in the center of town two days later. The tropical storm had given way to a cold front that covered Maine in eighteen inches of snow and sent the temperature plummeting to five degrees.

Wanda had a small insurance policy that covered her casket, plot, and burial. I sprang for the flowers so she could have gladiolas surrounding her at the funeral. A few people had bought wreaths for her that stood next to her casket.

I thought how Wanda would have found it amusing that, given her lifestyle, she was being buried in a white casket in a church.

I was worried that the church would be empty, but the place filled up so much that extra chairs had to be placed in the aisles. I guess that's small-town living for you.

The murders had attracted only a small amount of media

attention outside of Bridgetown. Ernie was fairly tight-lipped about the details of the crimes, which made it difficult for statewide and national news outlets to get the types of sound bites that sold newspapers. They were also distracted by the president's recent Twitter war with a few Middle Eastern nations. But that didn't stop news from spreading by word of mouth in town, with all sorts of rumors and variations to the story.

Joe Barrington stood in a pew by the side, looking like he wanted to wilt. Lorna wasn't with him, which I found interesting because she cared so much about outside appearances. Perhaps my attempt at shock therapy had given her the strength she needed to kick Joe to the curb.

Debbie Parks and Ernie Weagle stood next to me at the back of the church. They'd both apologized for doubting my innocence, but I couldn't really blame them. Doug and Renee had layered on the evidence against me.

"Nice," Ernie said, rubbing his chin and motioning toward me.

I decided to take Sheila's recommendation and do away with the beard altogether. I hoped I'd get used to being beardless, but I felt naked, as though something was missing.

"You were right, it was Doug's phone," Debbie whispered to me as the priest began speaking.

I shook my head, confused.

"Wanda called Joe Barrington from Doug's phone the night before."

"Joe must not have wanted to give up his phone."

She raised her eyebrows and shook her head.

"Their plan was to get you imprisoned, you know. Then kill Karen."

I thought about that for a moment, then mouthed, "How do you know?"

"It was in the notebook in his trailer," she whispered. "They'd been at this for at least a year."

I shook my head. My blind spots had almost let them complete their plan.

"Revenge for their daughter," Debbie said.

It bothered me that I would never know if Robert killed Madeline or if she killed herself. I told myself it didn't matter, and like Sheila said, there was nothing I could do. But it didn't sit right with me.

"You know that I didn't start the fire," I said.

"I know. I looked through the report. There were pieces of a notebook by the wood stove that might have started it."

"Yellow?"

She nodded.

Robert's official record. That must have been how Doug confirmed that I saw Robert.

"That's how he got my gun."

Debbie nodded discreetly.

"Will I get my gun back?" I said.

"It's evidence now. But I have to ask you, how did he get it out of the locker?"

"Don't even go there."

"I might have to issue an improper storage fine."

"I think I liked you better when you were serious."

After the Mass, I waited inside the church until it emptied so that I could speak to Randy. He was alone at the front of the church, sitting in the pew across from Wanda's casket. I approached him from the center aisle.

"Don't want to leave her alone?"

Randy took off his glasses and rubbed the bridge of his nose.

"She was a good sister."

I sat down next to him and crossed my arms, staring at the casket. "You know, I don't talk about my patients. I have this thing that what we talk about is sacred, secret. That I hold it in beyond the grave."

"I know."

I drew in a deep breath. "But Randy, I don't think she'd mind me telling you this. She adored you."

"Really?"

I nodded. I'd broken my rule, but perhaps some rules were made to be broken.

"Is it hard?" Randy said.

"What's that?"

"Keeping secrets."

I thought about that in light of the position Doug had put me in. "Well, it seems to be getting me into a bit of trouble. But why do you ask? Do you have a secret you want me to keep?"

He shook his head. "Not today, Doc."

I leaned back, relieved that no one wanted to confide in me right now.

"They say they might not be able to get her in the ground," Randy said. "Ground might be too frozen."

"Wait until spring?"

He shook his head. "We will have to cremate her and bury the ashes if need be."

"Why the rush?"

"The body has to be put to rest as quickly as possible. It's the Catholic way."

I nodded along, but I didn't understand. "What do you mean, the Catholic way?"

"Well, I believe, as do many Catholics, that at the end of days all bodies will rise from the grave to enter the Kingdom of Heaven."

"So if they're not in a grave?"

"They might not make it. And you never know when that day will come. So we bury our dead as quickly as possible."

The skin on my neck began tingling as Randy spoke. I quickly shook his hand, then ran out to my truck and headed for Vermont.

———

Jina looked out the window as Kurt Boone drove away. She waited a full minute before deciding it was safe to put down the shotgun.

She walked back to the sunroom, where Robert lay. As soon as he heard her footsteps, he turned his head.

"He's gone," she said.

"You're sure?"

She nodded.

He sat up and threw off his blankets, then grabbed a white towel beside the bed and wiped it over his face, pressing hard. It stained the towel yellow.

"This stuff is sticky," he said, trying to take off the makeup but leaving his face streaky.

"I think it's best if you have a shower," Jina said. "Use this too."

She gave him a large bottle of makeup remover.

He took it and gave Jina a hug. She wasn't sure she could let him go. She needed him too; he made her feel safe. But it wasn't safe for him anymore. She wished she could go back to their home, pick strawberries from the fields, and hold him with the security that it wouldn't be the last time.

"Hurry up, let's get going. We need to get you out of here."

26

The drive to Vermont was slow because the highways hadn't yet been plowed and salted. The tree branches were covered in a layer of light snow that glinted in the sun. One of my favorite things about the cold was that it brought stillness and calm.

I remembered the day I decided I needed to quit gambling for good. It was after a slushy, wet winter storm in Boston. It was six a.m., and I was walking back from an all-night poker game in a tanning studio, fresh off a hundred-thousand-dollar loss. I decided to detour through Copley Square when my shoelace got untied. I sat down on the bench to fix it when I saw two kids, a boy and a girl, in bright snowsuits gleefully jumping and rolling around in the snow. I watched them for a moment, but my eye was drawn to their father, who sat on another bench, just watching and absorbing the scene. I realized that I'd missed all of those moments with Karen, and vowed to make changes. And now I had a chance.

I stopped twice on the way to Jina Di Santis's home, first to pop into my office for my Sig Sauer in case things went south, and second to get some lunch. I grabbed an extra-large coffee on my way out, which lasted me the rest of the drive.

I arrived at Jina's house just before suppertime. The driveway was empty, with a single set of tire tracks in the snow and no garage, which meant she was out.

I parked and walked up to the door anyway, but there was no answer.

I got back in my truck, cranked the heat, and turned on country radio as I waited by the side of the road.

Even when I last met with Jina, I knew she was being evasive, but she gave me enough about Renee to allow me to find Karen before it was too late. That gave me hope that she would tell me the truth about Robert.

I'd been waiting forty minutes when Jina pulled up in her gray nineties Cadillac, seeming not to notice my truck by the road. She walked around the car, popped her trunk, and began pulling out groceries and shuttling them to her front step. Jina wore a long puffy jacket and maroon ankle-length skirt that touched the snow as she walked.

I cut the ignition, closed the door quietly, and walked up the driveway, my boots thudding against the snow.

"Need a hand?"

She startled as she turned around, reflexively putting a hand to her chest.

"Dr. Young. You scared me."

"Sorry about that."

I reached in the trunk, lifted the last two bags, and carried them to the door.

"I didn't think I'd see you again," she said, pulling her keys out of her purse.

"I was hoping we could talk. I had a few more questions."

She nodded softly and opened the door, then hung her coat up as I helped her carry the groceries to the kitchen.

"I'll deal with these later, thank you." She grabbed a glass from the cupboard, filled it with water, and drank it quickly. "It's so dry. Would you like a drink?"

"I'm fine, thanks."

"We can talk in the back."

I followed her to the sunroom and sat down on the couch as she took the armchair across from me and adjusted her skirt.

"Sorry to come unannounced," I said. "But I'm not sure if word got here yet. Kurt and Tori Boone are dead."

Jina's head tipped forward, and she stared at me as though she didn't quite believe me.

"It's true," I said.

She didn't speak for a long time, until finally she asked, "How?"

"Three days ago they were both shot."

"Really?"

I nodded.

Jina took a deep breath, exhaling as though she released half a decade of tension in a single breath.

"They tried to kill my friend and my daughter. But we stopped them. So Kurt Boone won't be bothering you anymore."

"Thank you."

"Well, I didn't really do it for you, Jina." I winked. "But you're welcome."

She cleared her throat and straightened up. I knew she would need some time to absorb the news, so I waited a few moments before continuing.

"I didn't come here to tell you that. I came here because until the last moment, the Boones insisted that Robert killed Madeline."

"He did not."

"Well then where did they get that idea?"

"I don't know," she snapped.

"Your son killed an innocent girl, Jina. And you're okay with that?"

"She killed herself. Because of her parents."

"What makes you so sure?"

"Because I just know my son!"

I leaned forward and put my hand on the armrest of Jina's chair. As I entered her personal space, she sank back in her chair.

"Let me tell you something, Jina, things that Robert might not have told you about me. I'm highly trained in human behavior and understanding the human mind. I know what people think because I can detect inconsistencies in their stories." I put my other hand on the armrest and looked at her squarely. "And I know you've been lying to me."

She uncoiled and slapped me across the face, then stood up and jabbed her finger at me.

"My Robert didn't kill anyone. Shame on you."

"Shame on me?"

She nodded, fire in her eyes.

"I almost lost the most important thing in the world to me because of your lies, Jina."

"No."

She crossed her arms and turned away from me.

"Because Robert's not dead, is he?"

"He's dead. How dare you?"

"He's not."

"Right there, right there." She pointed at an empty space in front of the wood stove. "He died right there, my boy. I miss him so much."

"Right there?"

"Yes." She pointed again.

I got up and walked past her toward the plate rail.

"Where are you going?" She moved toward me, but I boxed her out and grabbed the urn off the shelf.

"What are you doing?" she said.

I swiveled around, holding the urn in front of her. "Let me ask you, Jina, what kind of Catholic doesn't bury their child in the ground?"

"I want him here."

"No, I don't think that's why."

I started unscrewing the top. Jina reached for it, so I turned my back on her. She began pounding my head, but I was able to withstand the blows.

I unscrewed the top and looked inside.

Jina let go and brought a trembling hand to her face.

Inside the urn was a handful of small bills, what looked like a rainy-day fund.

"Tell me where he is."

"Nebraska?" Sheila said over Bluetooth.

"Red Cloud, population nine hundred thirty-two."

"And he's there?"

I was parked at the far end of a dusty grocery store parking lot, away from the other cars and carts. I'd driven through the night, almost without stopping, and made it to Nebraska in under twenty-four hours. Winter hadn't hit yet, so shoppers were still in T-Shirts and shorts.

"That's all I could get from her. He sends her letters without a return address, but he'd told her during a phone call once that was where he lived. She said in one of the letters he mentioned working at a grocery store, and there are only three in this town. I walked through two of them and didn't see him. So this is the third."

"What if she lied?"

"She didn't."

"You sure sound confident about that."

My mind was feeling clearer, and I sensed that my confidence was returning. "Pretty sure."

"Okay, and then what?"

"What do you mean?"

"What will you do if you find him?"

It was a good question, but one I wasn't ready to answer. The truth was the meeting with Robert could go many ways, and I had to be prepared for all of them. I looked at the passenger seat well to the case holding my Sig Sauer.

"Gus, he's gotten away with it. And he's still your patient... at least he was."

"I won't do anything stupid, if that's what you're asking. How's Karen?"

"Good. I was helping her set up her room at your place yesterday and..."

I saw him leave the store and pass ten yards ahead of me. He had aged more than I would have thought. His face was thin and narrow, with a bit of scruff that might have passed for a beard. Creases had formed around his eyes. He reached a red Toyota Yaris, took off his red and green smock, and tossed it on the passenger seat before getting in.

"Sheila, I'll call you back."

"Gus, just-"

I hung up before she could finish.

I pulled out of the parking lot, keeping about fifty yards back from the Yaris. I followed him through the main strip, past the typical assortment of small-town buildings, all with faded awnings shading their windows.

I didn't want to acknowledge it to myself, but Robert was responsible for Renee's and Doug's deaths. He almost caused

Karen's and Sheila's too. Jina insisted that he didn't kill Madeline, but that was immaterial to the fact that he had initiated a spiral nearly resulting in Doug and Renee destroying my life.

I wanted Jina to be right about Madeline taking her own life. My biggest fear as a shrink was that a patient of mine would kill someone and I failed to stop it. I'd never even considered the possibility that they would take my words as a directive to take another person's life.

He was in hiding, and that meant there was a real possibility he could become hostile when I confronted him.

He signaled left and turned down a flat dirt road flanked by yellow grassland. I followed him up the road until he pulled into a ranch-style home on a quarter acre of bare land.

I slowed as I approached. He walked up the dusty path to the house, unlocked the door, and went inside. I parked at the edge of his driveway.

I opened the gun case and contemplated leaving it behind. But I was about to blindside Robert, and a cornered cat was a dangerous creature. I grabbed the gun and attached the magazine, but I didn't load a round in the chamber before putting it in my jacket pocket.

I got out of the truck, closed the door quietly, and walked up to the door. When I knocked, Robert opened it.

"Hi, Robert."

Through the screen, his eyes were wide. He was trying to place me. "You're, you're-"

"The shrink you saw."

"How did you?"

"Your mom told me."

He leaned forward so his face was touching the screen. "What did you do to her?"

"Nothing, relax, nothing," I said. "Can we talk?"

He looked back, and I could hear the television playing. He unhooked the screen door and stepped outside onto the porch.

"The Boones are dead."

"Dead?"

"Yup. Both of them shot dead. So he won't come looking for you anymore."

Robert turned away and scanned the distance, as though expecting Kurt Boone to emerge from the horizon.

"He almost took my daughter, you know?" I said. "Revenge for his."

"Your daughter? Why?"

"Looks like you said something to him."

Robert pinched the bridge of his nose and winced. "I didn't mean for that to happen."

"But I can see where he was coming from, you know? Because if you take a man's daughter, well that's the most precious thing you can take."

"I, I know."

"I don't think you do. Not unless you are a parent. And almost lost a child."

Robert stepped across the porch and leaned against the railing. I thought he was going to say something, but he just stared out at the landscape. I could feel the tension radiating off him and put my hand on the gun handle in my pocket.

"Why did you do it, Robert?"

"No."

"I came all the way here. I need to know."

"You don't need to."

"Tell me why."

"I can't."

"Tell me!"

Robert abruptly turned and walked back to the door.

I thought about drawing the gun. Instead, I stepped between him and the door. "No, you don't get away that easy."

"Doc, it's okay." He raised his hands.

"You stay out here and tell me."

"Okay." He stepped back. "Okay."

I moved away from the door.

"Are you really alone?" he said.

"Yes."

"No one else?"

I shook my head.

Robert nodded and glanced toward the road again as though needing to confirm I was telling him the truth. "Maya, come here, sweetie."

A girl of about five burst out of the house. She wore overalls cut into shorts and had pigtails pointing out from both sides of her head. She looked at me with big brown eyes and smiled.

"Who's that man, Daddy?" she said.

"Just Daddy's friend." Robert leaned down and whispered something in her ear, and she ran around the house.

"Your daughter?"

Robert nodded.

"How old is she?"

"Gonna be turning six."

Maya returned in a woman's arms. The woman was tall, with a smooth, delicate face and braided long blonde hair. She wore a floral-patterned dress and walked barefoot. She had an interesting way of looking at me. Her eyes were on my face, but her gaze remained just off center so as not to make eye contact, as though she was afraid to. I wondered if this was learned from years of abuse.

"Madeline, this is Dr. Young."

She snapped her head toward Robert.

"Yeah, he's the one I went to see who helped us."

Her eyes finally met mine and she smiled, showing beautiful teeth.

"You're...you're here."

Madeline knelt down in front of Maya. "Sweetheart, why don't you go inside and watch some cartoons."

The little girl fist-pumped and ran back inside.

"Maddie, the doctor came to tell us something. Important."

Robert grabbed her hand and pulled her close as she looked at me, waiting.

"Madeline, your parents are dead."

Her jaw quivered, and I saw her eyes harden briefly before she broke from my stare.

"Really?"

I nodded.

"Do you want to come in?"

I spent an hour talking to Robert and Madeline at the kitchen table. Maya alternated between watching cartoons and skipping rope outside.

Robert did most of the talking while Madeline offered the occasional detail, but for the most part she stayed quiet. She let the more dominant one take the lead, as was beaten into her by her parents. Some habits die hard.

Robert had seen my name in the newspaper. I was testifying in a case of severe child abuse where a mother had thrown her four-year-old head first into a concrete wall. She refused to get the child medical attention, and he ended up dying from a slow brain bleed. The case was complicated because this family had been the subject of repeated child welfare investigations, and the child had been taken away before being returned to the mother. On the courthouse steps, a reporter asked me whether abusive parents should regain custody of their kids. I said, "What people need to understand is that in these cases the abuse becomes an addiction. And it's not the abuse per se that they are addicted to, it is the addiction to having control over another living being. And that addiction is almost impossible to beat."

He decided to get advice from me on how to help Madeline. He had intentionally left out her pregnancy because he was worried I would be more inclined to notify authorities and thought that would only put her at risk.

They met at the creek, Madeline without any shoes, and ran to Robert's home, where Jina had the car already packed and running. They drove to Harrisburg, Pennsylvania, where Jina's sister had an empty apartment for Madeline to stay. Jina cut Madeline's hair short and dyed it brown to help disguise her appearance.

Robert went back to New Hampshire and remained with Jina for several months. They tried to carry on as normal so the Boones wouldn't suspect him of having helped her escape. Kurt and Tori initially thought that Madeline was either abducted or ran away. They never filed an official missing person's report, which Robert believed was to avoid investigation of their treatment of Madeline. But that didn't stop Kurt from going to the media with his sob story.

It didn't take long for their suspicions to turn to Robert. Kurt Boone came to the house daily, demanding Robert tell him where Madeline was. Their suspicions increased when Robert told them that he had seen her trying to drown herself in the creek and assumed she was eventually successful. Tori Boone didn't believe that, and thought Robert was hiding something from them. The Boones began following Robert, parking in front of the home, obsessed with the idea that he had Madeline.

After Maya was born, Robert and Jina decided to move to

Vermont, hoping that Kurt and Tori would leave them alone. Their plan was to have Madeline and Maya move in with them.

But the Boones didn't stop, and Kurt and Tori soon located Jina's new Vermont home. Tori Boone arrived with a baseball bat one day and smashed both rear-view mirrors while demanding that Jina tell her where Maddie was. Madeline had hid in the basement holding Maya, waiting for Tori to leave.

Robert once again packed up the car, and Jina gave him the last of her savings for a down payment on a home in Nebraska. Robert took my words to heart, and decided to stage his death and confess to the murder so the Boones would stop searching.

It worked. At least the Boones left them alone. But they turned their rage to me.

I liked my solution better. It was more definitive.

———

Madeline and Robert waved from the edge of their driveway as I pulled away. I hadn't slept in over twenty-four hours, so I would need to spend the night somewhere. I thought maybe I would treat myself to a good night's sleep at a five-star in Chicago.

A phone call came through. Sheila.

"How'd that go?"

I looked out at the open road. It felt like I could see clearly for a thousand miles. It felt good.

"Sometimes, Sheila, things work out okay."

"I take it that it went well?"

"Very."

"Listen, you'll have to tell me all about it. But first, a new patient came in looking for help."

"Okay, sure."

Sheila exhaled into the phone.

"Are you sure you're ready for this one? It's a doozy."